MY BROTHER'S SHIELD

By : Link

This book is a work of fiction. Names, characters, places and incidents are products of the author's imagination and are not to be construed as real. Any resemblance to actual events, locales, organizations, or persons living or dead, is entirely coincidental.

COPYRIGHT

Orders by U.S. trade bookstores and wholesalers. Please contact Trient Press: Tel: (775) 996-3844;   or visit www.trientpress.com.
Printed in the United States of America
Publisher's Cataloging-in-Publication data LINK
A title of a book :My Brother's Shield
ISBN Hard Cover:978-1-953975-45-4
        Paperback: 978-1-953975-46-1
            E-book: 978-1-953975-47-8

DEDICATION

In thanks and gratitude for the people who've touched my life, this book is dedicated to you. John Lewis Crawford Jr, you welcome me into the neighborhood and took me in as your little brother. Your dad was my father in absence of my dad. You pushed me to improve my skills as an athlete when we were kids. Because of you, I joined the police department which led to a various career in law enforcement. Roxanne Carter and the Carter Family, thank you for your nurturing support in my adolescent years of growth.

To my mother Catherine, your stern guidance and nurturing kept me from being a slave to my environment. It was you who taught me diversity within diversity and knowing how to react with encounters from multiple ethnicity. Although your way of discipline is considered adverse by mainstream commentators of today, it kept me from being a victim to social injustice. To my siblings; we may live in different regions, but we're never too far apart.

To Toure, you reminded me of myself as a young man growing up. My professional dedication extends to those who served with me during my law enforcement career. Assistant Special Agent-In-Charge, Thomas Lynch, United States Secret Service of the Cleveland Field Office. Thank you for allowing me to serve upon your task force until I decided to leave.

To my OIU family: Betty Ford, Terence Taylor, Phil Langston Angela Dudley and Earl Mack. When I needed you, you were there. I can't forget about my allies from Cleveland PD-Narcotics, Strike Force, Vice and SWAT. My Brother's Blood is My Blood. For we all are a family in arms

PROLOGUE:

Some may say the first page of your book is the hardest to compose and others cold state of Ohio, an east coast city known as Cleveland. Many will state my home city is in the mid-west region, while others know it's an east coast place. The state of Ohio is broken up in three variations of geography. For example, the northwest part of Ohio is in the mid-west and the southern part is where the Mason-Dixon Line lies.

For those who are unaware of the Mason-Dixon Line, it separates the northern and southern states of the United States.   The imaginary line mentioned, travels through the City of Cincinnati, an Ohio City which sits adjacent to the Ohio River. Now earlier I mentioned Ohio was divided into three variations of geography and I've stated two already. The third geological place is the City of Cleveland. Cleveland sits three and a half hours from Buffalo, New York by travel of interstate ninety or I-90.

My city is known as a steel mill town, which is why many believed it to be in the mid-west. Now follow me closely as you read this statement I have written "a person's perception is their own belief whether their perceptions are true or false. Being taught this method of observation is how I accomplished the goals presented before me. Now, my goals changed as my life evolved and while my life was evolving, I changed as a person. Speaking of which, this is a great time to tell you about me.

I lived on the south side of Cleveland in a small neighbor known as Garfield Heights. Garfield was a segregated township with outspoken racism during my childhood. Half the kids in my "hood" went to Cleveland Public Schools, while others were privilege to a "Garfield Heights" educational system. The design segregation not only separated the opportunity to equal education, but further divided blacks against blacks. Oh, and forgive me for not using the term African American, but the mentioned term was not being used during my child hood. Trust me when I say this, because the term "Blacks" was more appreciative then other terms and analogies.   I lived on the "1-3-1", which is a mile from the inner-city of Cleveland. My area was injunctive to two choices, "gang banging and selling "dope" or play sports to achieve a scholarship for college. The mentioned choices sound easy, but the streets of Cleveland made it hard to choose. Choose your "homie" or choose your future. Stand by your family and live your dreams. Maybe your "homie" is your family, which causes you to postpone your dreams.

When I became a law enforcement officer, I was taught the four parables of being "Real Police".   The term "Real Police" was a title earned and not given because you wore a badge. The honor to be called "Real Police" was due to your integrity, fairness to the public and being consistent in doing your job. My first lesson was based off the parable "Downrange".   As an officer of "Downrange" you sacrifice everything for your brother and sister of your community as well as those in law enforcement.   Some would ask, why sacrifice for those of the community then those you serve with. Because the brothers and sisters of law enforcement you serve with have families in the community you protect.

My second lesson was base off the parable "I wear my Shield with Honor and Respect". This parable taught me how I should stand before my public. Let them see me as their shield that protects them, even if I must protect them from themselves.   My third lesson was from the parable "My brother's blood is my blood". When given an assignment with a fellow officer, I was taught my walk is not my walk alone. I fight the fight he fights and he fights the fight I fight. For his blood shed would be for my life, as my blood shed will be for his world.

My last lesson for "Real Police" indicated that a sworn officer wears his shield as a protector of his public, eliminating the wolf that preys amongst the weak and to never forget were you come from, because you will never see where you're going.

The contents of my book are fiction based from true life events. The characters of this book were created to illustrate my story.

CHAPTER ONE: THE BEGINNING

It was late fall of 1980, before a crowded college football stadium. The University North Central (UNC) is playing for bowl eligibility and to contend for the National Championship. The cheerleaders stood along the stadium track chanting fight songs to inspire their teams. You could also hear the school band playing in a distance, as the sound of screaming fans filled the stadium.   It's the fourth quarter of play and the strong college spirit continues as each team huddles up on the field. UNC quarterback gave instructions for the next play,

"Alright fellas', this is it! We need a first down to keep our drive alive." The Quarterback stated.

Each player joined hands to listen for their assignment. The team's broke formation of their huddles and line up from each other. They began shifting formations to keep each other off balance. UNC quarterback begins his cadence, looking over the defensive formation and trying to find the best match for his receiver. The ball is snapped into play, panning left to right, UNC quarterback is looking for an open receiver. He finally finds one on the right side of the field for a first down. The quarterback hurries his team to the line of scrimmage to snap and ground the ball. The official time clock stops, given UNC a shot to win this game.

UNC quarterback huddles his team for what seems to be their last chance of becoming bowl eligible. Fans begin screaming at the top of their lungs as UNC advances a first down.

"Ok fellas', let's make this count. It's win or go home... I-formation right, double screen on two...on two! UNC Quarterback instructed.

He breaks the huddle and hurries his team to the line of scrimmage. UNC Quarterback began shouting his cadence due to the loud screaming of opposing fans, "blue...22, 24, 16....hut-2-hike."

The ball was snapped into play, you could hear the grunting and colliding of pads as each player tries to advance one another. UNC quarterback releases a quick pass to his running back and he scampers fifteen yards for a first down. Fans continued cheering as time slips away.

The official score board read 29-seconds and counting in the fourth quarter. UNC quarterback signals everyone to line up for action, as he calls a play from the line of scrimmage. The score board read "first down and ten yards to go with UNC trailing 7-10.

Seconds continued to descend as UNC quarterback calls his play, "right….4-1-4, right….4-1-4, set red…blue 84; hut-2-hike."

The ball was snapped into play; UNC quarterback took a short drop into the pocket and scanned for an open receiver. He could feel his heart dramatically beating. The pocket began to collapse as his protection fell off, forcing him to elude tacklers and side-step defenders. As he continued to advance down field, his teammates provided blocks for him. Upon approaching the five- yard line and having one defender to beat, he leaped over the defender into the end zone. When the quarterback came to his feet, the game was over and UNC won 13-10.

The year is 2000, Detective-Sergeant James Jordan reminisces upon his victory performance as a college athlete at UNC. He stands in his living room looking at a team photo from UNC football; his son, Jim enters the room to engage in conversation.

"Having flash backs dad?" Jim asked.

"I guess you can say that. Dreams never die son. When I'm at the college watching you play, I see me…hoping you'll get that chance to play pro." James stated.

Jim walked over to the couch and sat down in a relaxed position. James dropped his head for a moment and then looked up at his son. Displaying a concern look upon his face, he exclaimed how his knee injury in college prohibited his pro football career. As James continued to speak, Jim interrupted.

"Dad what are you trying to say?" Jim asked.

"Stay away from the drugs and riff-raff going on in the streets." James answered.

Jim smiles as a sign of relief from what his dad had said. He then replies, "I thought it was something serious, not to say what you're trying to tell me isn't. I thought something was wrong. Now that I know there isn't, we can go eat mom's cooking."

Mrs. Jordan calls from the dining area, "dinner's ready."

James smile and says, "Let's go eat before your mom starts riffin'.

Jim chuckled at his dad's comment. "Riffin', when did you start speaking slang?"

"Since I began working at the Fourth District, all the young cops are talking it now," replied James.

James and his son, Jim, laughed as they both walked into the dining room for dinner.

Currently at the Fourth District of the Cuyahoga Police Department, night patrol was getting their assignments from their shift sergeant. The patrol room was filled with young officers ready to get their feel of the Cleveland street life.

"As you all know, tonight is not like any other night. Just a year ago we lost one of our own to a domestic altercation, which turn into a deadly shoot. My job is to make sure your ass' make it home every night. Therefore, be safe and try to keep the shootings to a minimum. Especially you Atkins, three shootings in one week is ridiculous." The shift Sergeant exclaimed.

Another officer chimed in on the sergeant's comment, stating Atkins was up to five killings due to a massacre the week before. Sergeant Connor redirected the officer's comment and continued his focus upon their assignments. Connor mentioned illegal betting was incurring on the college games in lieu of the "mom and pop" bars. One particular was identified as Club 1148 on Cleveland's west-side.

According to the sergeant's source, only the selected invited had unapproachable entry; other incomers had to be vouched for by a current member.

Officer Atkins interrupted the Sergeant's briefing by saying, "everyone bets on those games. Why do we have to get involved?"

The Sergeant replies, "Because it's illegal and the Mayor's office is on the Chief's back, which is causing him to chew on my white-ass. Look boys, contacts are down and we have a job to do. So quit your crying and let's pound some pavement. Oh, by the way, your hazard pay has been increased!"

Later at the Jordan's residence, the family sat down to have dinner. Kim speaks out in a rebellious tone to her mother. It seems Kim was in dislike of her mom's cooking. She even spoke bluntly of how terrible it was. "Mom, I am tired of having leftovers. It wouldn't be so bad if you would change it up a little. It's become monotonous, it really is," exclaimed Kim.

Mr. and Mrs. Jordan paused from eating their meal and looked over at their daughter. Their son Jim continued to eat as he knew his mother was about to bring the storm upon his sister.

"Girl, be thankful to have food upon this table and a roof over your sorry ass. Some families don't have a pot to piss in and a bed to shove it under. So, don't ever tell me you're tired of what I'm cooking. You can always open my front door and walk the FUCK out with no return. Trust and believe," exclaimed Mrs. Jordan.

Jim looked up from his plate to see what was going to be said next. Right then, Mr. Jordan (James) interrupted to break the flow of conversation. He excused Kim and Jim from the table, asking his son to take Kim to the store and bring back some ice cream. Mr. Jordan then turns his attention to his wife after the kids left the room.

"Pam, you didn't have to go two feet in the chest on her." Jordan stated.

Mrs. Jordan scoffed and then replied, "Kim needs to know her place. Just because she's fourteen years old and has a period, doesn't mean she can have an opinion about my cooking.

Jim and Kim were in the living room gathering their coats from the closet. They could hear the low murmur of their parent's voices as they continue to talk in the kitchen.

Jim comment to his sister about her behavior at the dinner table. "Girl, you're lucky to still have your lips on that face."

Kim states, "I don't know why she's acting like I'm making shit up?

Jim replied, "What? You practically said her cooking isn't shit."

Kim sighs and refuses to accept accountability for her actions, while her brother continues to rant about the disrespect she exhibited.

"Last time I said something close to your shenanigans, I was looking at the ceiling from my back. Jim stated.

Kim replies, "I don't care!"

Jim shook his head at the comment Kim made. He then stated, "Yeah, you're young minded. You will understand one day."

Mr. Jordan then walks into the living room. He gave Jim money for ice cream and said, "Look, here's $5.00 for a half gallon of ice cream. Butter Pecan is the flavor for the night and be sure to bring back my change." Mr. Jordan turns to Kim and kisses her on the forehead.

Jim and Kim left their home to buy ice cream as instructed by their father. As they headed down the driveway onto the sidewalk, Jim commented on how he was keeping the change after purchasing ice cream.

"Dad thinks he's getting his change back. I don't think so." Jim stated.

"Don't bring back dad's change, and its la-la bye Jimmy. You hear me playa?" Kim replied.

"You just mad about mom getting in your mix." Jim rebuttal.

Kim chuckles as they walk to the store. Kim began talking about her brother's football future. "You think you'll go pro?" Kim asked. "Dad thinks so and I want to...but you know dad, he's living his dreams through me. I see the enthusiasm he has for me to make it." Jim stated.

As Jim and Kim walked closer to the neighborhood store, a white delivery van pulled in front of its entrance. The van's side door open and two unidentified gunmen exited the vehicle. The gunmen entered the store in attempt to rob the store keeper. Unknown to the assailants, an on-duty police officer was in the store buying snacks.

"How much are these small donuts?" The Policeman asked.

"$0.69 for a pack of six and $1.25 for a twelve pack." Sal, the Store Keeper replied.

One of the gunman yells, "Face down on the fucking floor and don't move.

The police officer's position was shielded from the gunmen's view. The officer pulls his weapon and tries to gain a position to ambush the gunmen. Sal complies with the gunmen orders and lies face down upon the floor. As the officer closes in on the position of the gunmen, he steps on a peanut shell and create a crackling sound. The startling noise gives the officers location away. One of the gun man turns towards the officer direction and began firing a small compact semi-automatic weapon. The gunman's bullets sprayed throughout the store as the officer return fire, striking one of the gunmen. Unsure of the officer's location, the gunmen disengaged and ran out of the store. Jim and Kim heard the shooting as they approach the store front entrance. Kim stood six feet away from her brother as the gunmen exited the store. The officer pursued closely behind the assailants as they exited store. He stopped and stood at the store entrance, firing his weapon at the gunmen. One of his bullets inadvertently struck Kim causing her to fall lifelessly to the ground. The van pulls off into the night with screeching tires and a cloud of smoke.

The officer stood before Kim's body, yelling on his police radio for emergency assistance. He then looks over in Jim's direction and see him lying upon the ground as well. The bullet which struck Kim exited her body and pierced Jim. You could hear the distant sound of emergency vehicles becoming louder and louder. People begin to crowd the area as police and emergency medical services arrived on scene.   Jim looks over at his sister's body, her eyes open as she lay in a pool of blood.

"No, no, no! She can't die. She can't die...my sister can't die!" Jim screamed.

A paramedic rushes to Jim's aid to assist his injuries. Jim watch the other paramedics on scene cover Kim's body. Jim could see the EMT's lips moving, but could not hear the words from their mouths. Suddenly, he could hear the EMT attending his injuries speaking to him.

"Son, are you okay?" Paramedic #1 asked.

Jim cries out, "I've been shot. Oh God, it hurts. Is my sister okay?"

"Try not to talk. We're trying to contain the bleeding. C'mon, let's get him out of here," said Paramedic #1!

The paramedics loaded Jim's body upon a gurney and placed him into the ambulance.   As the ambulance drove off, police personnel continue to work the crime scene.

On this same night and thirty minutes from this horrific scene, another tragic incident was about to unfold. The Grahams were pulling into the parking lot of a Dairy Mart. The listed premise was located in an all-white neighborhood on Cleveland's west-side. Mr. Graham and his son, Terrell exited their vehicle to enter the Dairy Mart. They observed several police vehicles sporadically parked with emergency lights displaying. Mr. Graham told Terrell to keep walking and pay no attention to the officer's outside of the store. The officer's outside of the store looked over at Terrell and his dad, as they both walked into the store.

The frantic innkeeper looks up at the Graham's upon them entering his store. He then utters the phrase, "That's them officers!!"

A uniform officer ordered Terrell and his dad to stop. Terrell was caught off guard and questioned the officer as to why he ordered them to stop. The officer replied in a discourteous tone, requesting Terrell to be quiet. Unhappy with the officer's tone as he spoke to Terrell, Mr. Graham then spoke against the officer's authority.

"You don't have to speak to my son that way." Mr. Graham evoked his opinion.

The officer looks over at the store manager for confirmation of identity. Mr. Graham reaches into his coat to retrieve his Identification and in just seconds, the officer fired his service weapon. The bullet from the officer's weapon strikes Mr. Graham in the chest. Terrell lets out a loud scream as his dad fell to the floor. The officer walks over to Mr. Graham's body to notice him holding his ID in hand.

"Where's the gun...I saw a gun." The officer shouted.

Additional officers entered the store after hearing gun shots. Terrell stood in shock, watching his father bleed out on the store floor. The sound of his beating heart over took the surrounding auditory effects. Terrell could see the officer's lips moving, but their words weren't registering to his brain. Upon being thrown to the floor and handcuffed, Terrell began to listen to what was happening around him.

"What the hell happen?" Arriving officer asks.

"I thought he was reaching for a gun. The store manager identified them as the suspects," stated the officer who shot Mr. Graham.

"That can't be true, car #54 arrested the suspects five minutes ago. Who identified them as suspects?" Arriving officer asks.

"The store manager," replied the officer who shot Mr. Graham.

The arriving officer transmits on his police radio, requesting an ambulance to their location. Tears began falling from Terrell's eyes, as distant police chatter took over the scene.

The sound of a landline phone rings out in the Graham's home. Mrs. Graham answers the phone. She hears the whimpering voice of her son, Terrell. She asks him what is wrong and in a crying voice, Terrell utters his father was dead. Mrs. Graham sits softly onto her couch and stared into the phone. At this time, her younger son "Mookie" walks into the room. Mrs. Graham places the phone back to her cheek and asks Terrell, where was he?

"I'm at Mount Sinai Hospital with dad's body." Terrell replied.

Mrs. Graham told Terrell she would be right there as the call ended. Mookie walks over to his mother, questioning and asked the sad look upon her face. She tells him his father has been murdered by the police. In disbelief; Mookie asks his mother what happen, but she's unable to put together complete sentences. Mookie embraces his mother as they consoled one another.

Meanwhile at Mount Sinai hospital, a police officer guards the door area of Jim's room as he lay unconscious in bed. Mr. Jordan is sleeping in a chair next to him when he hears his son whimpering. He immediately opens his eyes and smiles, relived to see his son conscious again. Jim grunts from pain of his injuries. The doctor walks in to attend to Jim's discomfort and conduct a post assessment. Jim looks at him and asks about his sister. A tear falls from Mr. Jordan's eye as the doctor tells Jim his sister is dead. Jim loved his sister so dearly; his eyes became flooded with tears as he fell back upon his bed.

Three days passed before Jim was released from the hospital. The Friday of his release from care, Jim's parent brought him home. While at home, two Cuyahoga Police Detectives visited his home. They questioned Jim about the incident which took his sister's life. The CPD detectives asked did he or his sister have any known enemies.

"Enemies, the person who shot my sister and I was a cop." Jim stated in anger.

The detective redirected his question and asked, "What were you doing at the store?"

Jim answered, "We were going to buy ice cream…the flavor of that night was Butter Pecan."

"Ok, I see...our questioning here is done for now. Get some rest and we'll be in touch," stated one of the detectives.
The two detectives then left the Jordan's home.   Jim wasn't satisfied with his sister's death investigation. He was certainly annoyed with how the detectives were trying to display the blame.

"I need to reach out to the streets. Someone knows something and I 'tend to find out what."   Jim thought to himself.

CHAPTER TWO: MEET YOUR PARTNER

Monday afternoon, three days after CDP detectives visited the Jordan's home, Jim met up with his cousin Pete at the corner store where Kim was killed. They talked about the shooting and possibilities of why it wasn't an accident.

"Why do you say Kim's death wasn't an accident, asked Jim?

Pete looks at Jim, pausing before answering his question. Impatient as he is, Jim asks' Pete to clarify his statement about Kim's death. Pete gave a big sigh and finally answered Jim's question.

"It was an opportunity to collect on a hit. Your sister had a green light on her." Pete Answered.

Why her, asked Jim?

"Outside selling dope, HHK (Harvard Heights Kings) is into collection for illegal gambling operations. They even have a few CPD (Cuyahoga Police Department) cops on the payroll." Pete replied.

"I get the drug and gambling part with HHK, but why kill Kim?" Jim asks.

"Kim found out about it and with Uncle James being a cop, they felt she was a liability. That cop, the one who killed Kim, he works for HHK." Pete explains.

Jim eyes became watery and red as fire upon hearing why his sister was killed. Jim was a person who processed things systematically and moved in accordance. He pledged to play in Saturday's big game against their conference rivals. CSU (Cuyahoga State University) has never been a contender for the National Championship. Jim knew his school had chance to make their first college bowl appearance and he didn't want his sister's death to be a distraction. He vowed to deal with HHK and CPD, thereafter.

Later that week on a Saturday afternoon, the stadium was filled completely with little standing room. Proceeding kick-off, Jim's team begin play at their own 45-yardline. It was at this moment the star quarterback of CSU displayed how valuable he was to his team. Jim opened with a strategic air assault, facilitating designed plays to keep the opposing team off balance. Jim's defense dominated their opponents, which allowed him to "show-boat" for the fans. He threw touchdown after touchdown until the score read 42-0. Before the game ended, Jim led his team into the end zone twice more, finalizing the score to read 56-0. The blow out offset the local betting in Cleveland, causing interested parties to sustain severe losses of dividends.

After the game, Jim went to meet his cousin Pete at "Lancer's", a known restaurant that served great "Seafood and Steak." Lancer's was also known for appearances by celebs who started their careers in Cleveland. As Jim arrived, he noticed CPD police cars in front of Lancer's and yellow police tape being put up. Leaning towards the nearest by-stander, Jim asked what happen.

"Someone was killed inside." The by-stander replied.

"Who's the victim?" Jim thought to himself.

Jim witnessed the coroners bringing a body bag from inside Lancer's. A CPD officer stops the gurney to open the body bag. As the officer took a photo of the decease, Jim saw the victim to be his cousin Pete. He couldn't believe what he'd seen. Tears of sorrow became Jim's tears of avenging anger. He stood there with anger in his heart and the urge to kill in his eyes.

Three years later, it was a Saturday night and the anniversary of Pete's death. Jim found himself at the front door of "Kraus's Gentlemen's Club." The listed premises were known for prostitution and illegal gambling. Retired CPD Detective, Mark Kraus own the establishment. The questionable methods of this detective landed him in bed with Cleveland Politicians who condone illicit acts.

Jim entered and found a vacant seat at the bar. Madam Mae sat an empty glass in front of him.

"What are you having?" Mae asks.

"Double shot of Vodka on the rocks and a splash of water." Jim stated.

"Looking for some action?" Mae asks.

"Yes", replied Jim!

"Well name your pleasure!" Mae stated as she displayed herself.

Jim scoffed, giving Mae a smirking-grin as he looked her in the face. He displayed a steady and long stare, causing Mae to feel uneasy of his presence. Jim's silence seemed forever to Mae, but only seconds had elapsed. He then stated, "Not you bitch...Where the fuck is shorty?

Staring back into Jim's face, Mae nodded her head sideways towards a door leading to the upstairs of this establishment.   Jim threw back his drink and headed towards the door.

Opening the door and creeping quietly to the top floor, Jim could hear the faint voice of a woman moaning softly. The sounds of her voice became louder as he walked the narrow hallway. Coming upon a door to his immediate right, he could hear a bed frame squeaking and the sounds of woman moaning. Suddenly Jim heard another voice. It was the voice of a man he'd been searching for. Jim gently open the door and walked inside while the couple was having sex.

"SHORTY!" Jim shouted.

Shorty turned to look over his shoulder and was met with a bullet to his forehead. Brain fragments from Shorty's injuries landed upon the woman's face. Jim exited the room, heading back to the main floor of the establishment. Before leaving the gentlemen's club, Jim discharged his weapon in the air.

"This is for my sister and cousin Pete." Jim shouted.

Jim ran out the side entrance into adjoining business parking lot. He could hear sirens approaching the front entrance of Kraus' club as he ran into the dark. Moments later, Jim could see in a distance the flashing blue lights from Cuyahoga Police units. Jim continued running and disappears into the Cleveland night.

The next morning at Calvary Cemetery, James Jordan and his wife Pam visited their daughter's grave site. Jim arrived moments later to join his parents.

"I miss you baby," Pam spoke onto her daughter's grave as a tear flowed down her right cheek.

Jim stood in solace, reflecting on the night before. James Jordan fell to his knees, whimpering for the loss of his daughter. Placing his hand upon his father's shoulder and hugging his mom, Jim consoled his family. He kept playing the doctor's voice over and over in his head.

"Your sister didn't make it. She was dead when the ambulance arrived. There was nothing they could have done." Echoed the doctor's voice in Jim's head.

Jim starred at his sister's headstone as he continued hugging his family.   Unknown to the Jordan's, someone was watching them from a far. The unknown subject shielded his presence behind a near tree, while taking photos of Jim and his family. The subject then retrieves a cellphone and places a text message to another party.

"They have no clue, but I'll keep close tabs on them." The text message read.
The unknown subject put away the cellphone and continues taking photos of the Jordan's.

Before departing Kim's grave site, Pam says a small prayer for her family. "Dear Lord, we ask for your forgiveness, your continued blessing upon our family. This beautiful soul in which you've taken, keep her safe until we all can meet again. Please keep the heavily gates open for my family and I...Amen!"

The subject in the shadows continues his photographing of the Jordan's as they stood by Kim's grave site.

Later that afternoon at Cuyahoga Police District #4, Police Detectives of Homicide and their Captain were debriefing facts about the shooting at Kraus' Gentlemen's club.

"What details do we have on last night shooting, questioned the Captain?

Sir, we interviewed the female barmaid name Lucinda Vixen who goes by name Vix." She stated the assailant's face was covered by his hoodie, stated Detective #1.

"How did she know it was a male-perp?" The Captain asks.

"I asked that same questioned Cap, and she stated the subject's broad shoulders caught her attention." Detective #1 stated.

"Any further descriptions made by the witness? Captain asks.

"The witness was reluctant to give further descriptions, claims everything happen too fast." Detective #2 implied.

"Look! We all know this 'trick' knows more than she's giving up. Put a tail on her and let's see where it leads. Somethings tells me she knows more than she's indicating. Keep in mind gentlemen, "Mark Kraus" has deep connection in city politics. Therefore, tread lightly with this one and bring some results in fast!" The Captain stated. The Captain concluded his briefing with the detectives.

Currently downtown at Cuyahoga Police Headquarters, Detective-Sergeant James Jordan was summoned to the Chief's office. As Sergeant Jordan walks into the Chief's office, he observed an undesirable person in the room. Joining the meeting was Detective-First Grade, Tim Carter. Detective Carter was the pessimist from CPD-Gang Unit. Everything which could go wrong usually had his name written on it.

"Please...come-in." Chief Jenkins asks.

Detective Carter turns to Sergeant Jordan's direction pauses and then turns back towards the Chief. Carter leans over to the Chief's desk and begins to speak in a soft whisper.

"You got to be fuckin' kidding me." Carter Whispers.

The Chief whisper's back, "Listen, to what I have to say."

Sergeant Jordan walk's over to the Chief's desk and stood adjacent from Carter. Chief Jenkins clears his throat! He then explains why Jordan and Carter were in his office. Jenkins informed the detectives they were his new intelligence team, supporting homicide and violent crime investigations. He further referred to this unit as "Hazardous Targets Section or HTS.

"Detective-Sergeant Jordan, meet your new partner." Jenkins stated.

Jenkins extended his hand towards Detective Carter as a gesture of identification. Detective Carter began shaking his head in disbelief. Sergeant Jordan chuckles at Carter's dissatisfaction. Jenkins outline the detective's duties, giving them unapproachable authority to investigate old and new homicides. Detective-Sergeant Jordan saw this as an opportunity to look deeply into the cold case of his daughter's death.

Currently outside and across the street of Police headquarters, sat two thuggish-appearing black males in a parked van. The occupying males are identified as T-Bone and High-Top, gang members of the Harvard Heights Kings. They were listening to gangster-style rap music and watching the front entrance door of police headquarters. T-Bone lights up a marijuana cigarette and takes a puff, blowing smoke from his mouth and inhaling it back into his nose. High-Top looks over at T-Bone to observe him enjoying the sensation of being high.

"I hate sitting in one spot too long." High-Top stated.

"Don't sweat it, this shit will be over soon enough. Besides, we have a job to do and we can't leave until it's done!" T-Bone replied.

"Still, I don't like being a sitting duck. Let me hit that joint fool!" High-Top demanded.

T-Bone passes the marijuana cigarette to High-Top. High-Top takes a puff and coughs a little bit. He then takes another puff and exhales the smoke from his nose. Suddenly, the two gang members observed Sergeant Jordan and Detective Carter exiting Police Headquarters.

"There's our target." High-Top stated.

T-Bone rises up in the driver seat and starts the van. The van idles while T-Bone holds their position. Unknown to T-Bone and High-Top, a mystery person is taking photos of their van. The unknown person sees T-Bone looking in the direction of Jordan and Carter. The two detectives were arguing about the Chief paring them together.

"I am sick of the chief chewing my ass over simple shit," Carter stated.

Jordan chuckles at Carter's comment. He then replies, "I would be too! You white boys don't have much to start with."

Carter then states, "That's what I'm talking about. You're never serious."

"I have more serious nerves in my body then you'll ever know. Since my daughter's death, I've become more serious than ever. That's an insult, coming from a person who's been caught in more fucked-up shit then anyone. You should take working with me as a privilege." Jordan stated.

The mystery person began taking photos of Jordan and Carter during their minor quarrel. While Jordan was in Carter's face, the van occupying T-Bone and High-Top made a U-turn towards the detective's location. High-Top sticks the barrel of his shot gun outside the passenger window. As he's about to pull the trigger, their van crashed into a parked vehicle. High-Top looked over at T-Bone and found him to be slumped over the steering wheel. High-Top lifted his friend's head and noticed a bullet hole in his forehead. Blood was protruding from the wound and dripping onto the steering wheel. Another bullet flew out in silence, striking High-Top in his temple and causing his body to collapse immediately.

The mystery person places an AR-15 assault rifle with a silencer upon the front seat of his vehicle. He then starts his vehicle and drives away unnoticed. Startled by the disturbance, Jordan and Carter stops their bickering to investigate the crash. Upon their approach of the van, they noticed the collapsed bodies of High-Top and T-Bone. Several more officers came over to assist, while other police personnel directed vehicle traffic and taped off the scene. Jordan and Carter starred at one another as sounds of in distinctive chatter and emergency sirens falls into the background.

CHAPTER THREE: LOST LOVE

It's 8:00 p.m. on a brisk and clear night. Jim enters the Euclid Towers apartment complex, located in the City of East Cleveland. As he walks through the front lobby, Jim gives the desk clerk a nod and continues to the elevator area. He presses the call button, signaling a car to his location. Seconds later, the elevator doors open and Jim enters. He then presses another button signaling the eight-floor as his destination.

The elevator car arrives at the eight-floor. Jim exits and walks to apartment #802. He adjusts his clothes to assure a good appearance before knocking. The sound of three knocks amplified from the door. A female voice softly answers from the other side. She then opens the door, displaying a beautiful smile.

"Hey baby," said Jim.

The female replies, "It's about time you came to attend the needs of your woman."

"I didn't know I had to report my every move." Jim stated.

"You're lucky I love your sexy ass. Now come and kiss me." His woman replies.

Jim complies with his lady wishes. Kissing his woman aggressively and discarding her clothes to the floor, Jim picks his lady up and carries her into the bedroom.

Jim laid his girlfriend onto the bed and whisper's, "I love you Tina."

Jim's admiration of Tina's body causes his penis to erect for pleasure. He then undresses himself and the couple began making love, showing each other deep exotic pleasure. Throughout the night, the couple enjoyed multiple positions of pleasure. At one point, Tina could feel the excretion of Jim's semen hitting her vagina walls. The sensation drives Tina wild and causes her to experience countless orgasms. She begins to let her body be free in the event of love making, excreting fluids of her own until the bed was completely wet. Tina moan's with intense pleasure, enjoying the insertion and extraction of Jim's penis. She enjoyed it so much; Tina straddled Jim's body for one more orgasmic ride. The two fell asleep in each other arms, Tina on top and Jim underneath.

The next morning, Jim awakened to sunlight shining through Tina's bedroom window. He could smell coffee brewing and sausage cooking. Rising from the bed, Jim enters the kitchen naked. Jim's presence causes Tina to turn around and focus upon his manhood as she smiles at him.

"I prefer your sausage without any sides." Tina said.

Jim chuckles at Tina's comment. He then walks over to the breakfast table next to the terrace window. Tina walks over to Jim and kisses him upon his lips. She then turns her back towards him and bends over the breakfast table, inviting Jim to penetrate her from behind. Jim rises to attention and presses his body against Tina's ass. The two moved in sequence together, causing a rhythmic motion of pleasure.

As they continued to make morning love, Jim hears glass breaking and feels the warmth of Tina's brain matter on his chest area. He steps backwards, watching Tina's lifeless body fall to the floor. Jim then looks through the terrace window and sees a man on an adjacent rooftop of another building. The Un-sub is recharging his rifle for another shot, but Jim takes cover on the floor of Tina's apartment. The rifleman looked through his scope, searching for Jim's existence. Unable to locate him, the rifleman secured his weapon and exited the rooftop. Jim kept still for moments, hoping the gunman had left the area.

Jim crawls to the bedroom, shielding himself from the window's view. He then began searching for his clothes to get dress. Meanwhile, the un-sub makes his escape to an idling black Cadillac CTS. He enters the front passenger seat and the vehicle drives off, baring Ohio License plate #HHK4LF. Minutes later, Jim exits the Euclid Towers onto a back alley, which lead him to the 1800 block of Charles Street. He never wanted anyone at Euclid Towers to know what kind of vehicle he drove.

Jim parking on Charles Street was perfect to his escape without being noticed. He enters his car and leaves the area without further incident.

Meanwhile on the south eastside of Cleveland, ODI (Ohio Department of Investigations) Agents and local CPD officers were gearing up for a tactical raid. Suggested target location was the intersecting block of East 175th street and Tarkington Road.   Special Agent Ford of ODI and Captain Williams of CPD debrief one another.

"What's the plan of action," asked Agent Ford?

"Patrol will set up a two-block radius, seizing foot and vehicle traffic. Three teams will approach the target location on foot. As we know, no neighbors are at home. Civilian casualty should be zero percent." Captain Williams replied.

Agent Ford nodded her head in agreement with the operation plan. Her team of covert agents and CPD officers geared up for entry. Agents of ODI were in full blacked out tactical gear to mask their identity during overt interactions. Agent Ford instructed joint enforcement teams to engage the location of 7225 E.175th Street. Team one safe guarded the perimeter as teams two and three entered the home. At the command of Agent Ford, flash grenades were projected into the home with intent to cause disorientation and mental paralyses to occupants inside.

"Police, police, get on the floor," shouted by officer's as the cleared areas of the home. Concluding the search and securing of subjects found in the home, law enforcement personnel began questioning detainees.

"I need to see the owner of this house!" Agent Ford requested.

A CPD detective brought forth an Arabic woman to Agent Ford's attention.   Agent Ford asked the woman was she the owner of the home. The woman spoke in Arabic dialect as to evade questioning. Agent Ford redirected her line of questioning, this time in Arabic. The woman eyes widen in surprise of Agent Ford's ability to speak Arabic. Ford continued her questioning of the female suspect. Concluding their conversation, Agent Ford had the woman taken to a secure location for further questioning. Captain Williams and his team remained on scene to complete their investigation.

In his Cleveland Heights apartment, Jim sits on the couch thinking of Tina and their last moments together. He then turned his focus to a female news reporter on television. She reports the breaking news of a woman found dead in her East Cleveland apartment. Jim knew Tina's death would soon lead back to him. He needed to contact his dad, Detective-Sergeant James Jordan. "My father would know what to do," Jim thought to himself.

Currently at the scene of Tina's homicide, Detective-Sergeant Jordan is investigating her death. Combing through unsubstantiated evidence and assessing probabilities of the scene, Sergeant Jordan tries to identify his suspect. Detective Carter arrives on scene to assist his partner.

Sergeant Jordan was kneeling next to the deceased. He then looks up at Detective Carter and states, "Nice of you to show up!"

"I was caught up in a thing. Nothing you would understand!" Carter replied.

Jordan stares at Carter for a second and then began to brief him about the investigation. Carter began examining the body and found a clue to their investigation.

"Hello?" Carter said in a puzzled voice.

"What do you see?" Jordan asked.

"She's leaking fluids," said Carter. He then pointed at the discharge of fluid leaking from Tina's vagina.   "We might have a suspect after all," concluded Carter.

Sergeant Jordan ordered a Crime Scene Investigator to swab the decease vaginal area. "Rush that sample through the lab. I want to know who saw Ms. Lopez a live last," expressed Sergeant Jordan.

The detectives departed Tina's crime scene. Carter advised Jordan he wanted to check on another lead before meeting him at headquarters. Jordan head-nodded Carter and entered his vehicle to drive off. While in route to HQ, Jordan played the evidence over in his head. He was trying to connect the dots for a suspect or possible witness.   Upon arriving to HQ, Sergeant Jordan went to his desk and began searching facts from the crime scene.

Detective Carter enters HQ moments later and was immediately summoned to the Chief's Office. "You wanted to see me sir," asked Detective Carter.

"Sit down Carter," replied Chief Jenkins. Jenkins was looking at the news report of Tina's death. It seemed every local station was chimed in on her demise. "News stations are reporting by the hour about the homicide at Euclid Towers. You would think this woman was some type of celebrity." Chief Jenkins stated.

"You have no idea," stated Carter.

"What do you mean genius?" Jenkins asks.

"She's the daughter of current Liquor Commissioner, Constantine Gordon. The victim uses her mother's maiden name of "Lopez" to not be associated with her father political career and mob constituents." Carter exclaimed.

Chief Jenkins starred off into the air with a puzzled look. He knew this would be more of a political extravaganza than a homicide to investigate.

Meanwhile in the Bureau of Hazardous Targets Section, Jordan was reading the notes of his daughter's cold case. For some reason he felt his daughter's death and Ms. Lopez murder were connected. Jordan had no clue the connecting piece was his son. As he continued to read the case notes, his eyes began to water and turn bloodshot. Jordan drifted back in thought of Kim's funeral service. Reminiscing the Pastor's spiritual passage, "Dirt is what you are created from and dirt shall you return as the earth inhabits your body. May the gates of Heaven welcome your soul as it rests in peace. " Suddenly, Jordan snapped back to current time and noticed Detective Carter standing before him.

"We got work to do. Let's go!" Carter stated.

"Do you have a lead?" Jordan asked.

"I do! We have to wait until dark." Carter replied.

Later that evening, Jordan and Carter were staking out the city towing yard for clues. While conducting their surveillance, Jordan began reminiscing upon the night he identified his daughter's body. The vision of that night played over and over in Jordan's head until the current voice of Detective Carter, interrupt's the loop.

"Jordan," shouted Carter.

"Huh, what?" Jordan replied.

"I thought you sleeping with your eyes open." Carter stated.

"Nah, just thinking," answered Jordan.

"Right, well this tow yard is where T-Bone use to work. According to my informant, he also stayed at the Daily Rental next to it." Carter explained.

The rental Detective Carter was speaking of was a rent-a-room motel for transient occupants. A lot of prostitutes and pimps used the dump as a platform for business. The two detectives exited their vehicle and began walking towards the premises.

"Why are we looking into this dump? I thought Robbery-Homicide was investigating this case?" Jordan asks.

"They are! The van T-bone was found dead in happen to be at the scene of your daughter's death." Carter stated.

Jordan paused and displayed a look of confusion in response to Carter's comment. He then gathered his composer and entered the motel with Carter. The faint sound of a tiny bell jingles as the detectives open the entrance door. As they approach the desk clerk, Sergeant Jordan takes out his badge to identify himself.   He then asked the desk clerk what room was occupied by Terence Barham. The desk clerk examined Jordan's badge and identification.

"I never heard of him." The Clerk stated.

"He also goes by the name T-Bone." Jordan replies.

Carter then leans towards the desk clerk and says, "Val is your name, right?

The desk clerk looks at Jordan and then back at Carter, nodding her head to answer yes. Carter then draws in a sniff and leans more into the clerk's personal space. He wanted the clerk to take his presence serious as he gave her an ultimatum.

"Val or whatever the fuck you want to be called, I can go to my squad car and request an electronic warrant to search this entire dump. It's no telling what I might find to arrest your White-Lillie-Ass for. I suggest you retrieve the room keys!" Carter demanded.

Val retrieves the keys as requested and hands them to Detective Carter. Carter blows a kiss at Val in disrespect, as he and Jordan leaves to inspect the room rented by T-Bone. In a last minute of utterance, Val tells detectives T-Bone also hung out at the pool hall on Miles Avenue and 131 Street. Sergeant Jordan nods his head as an indication to say thank you.

As soon as the detectives had cleared the lobby, Val picks up the desk phone and called an unknown party to inform on the detectives at her motel. The open line rings three times before the unknown party answers.

"Hello," answered the mystery person.

"It's Val, those cops you told me about are here. They are up in T-Bones room looking for something." Val stated.

"Good, make sure they have no trouble of getting what they need." The mystery person replied.

Val terminates the call and returns to her desk duties.

Thirty minutes later, Jordan and Carter exit's the Daily Rental Motel. They were unable to find any evidence linking T-Bone's murder to Lopez'. Puzzled as to why Carter suggested to inspect the Daily Rental Motel, Jordan questioned his motives.

"Why're you so sure T-bones and Lopez' murders are connected?" Jordan asks.

"Father Terry!" Carter replied.

Father Terry also known as Terry Oranthal Junior was a half Black-Italian who turned clergyman due to his exile from the Cleveland Mob. Local mobsters considered him as an impure Italian because of his bloodline. However, federal law enforcement listed Terry as the next lethal mob boss. Unsubstantiated facts suggested he was using his church to launder illicit funds through church ties. Although it hasn't been proven, state and federal agencies kept his name on their watch list.

"Father Terry does a lot for the black community," stated Jordan.

"You mean through that organized crime temple he calls a church in Garfield Heights." Cater replies.

"Don't be a fucking jerk. When I was a kid, St. Terry's Catholic Church funded our little league football team. That team helped a lot of kids! If it wasn't for his support, kids in my hood wouldn't had a choice. Shit, I probably would've been an HHK member myself. I can't believe that hype about Father Terry and St. Terry's Catholic Church." Jordan exclaims.

Jordan stood by the driver-side of their police vehicle and began thinking about his playing days for St. Terry All-star's. Seconds later, Carter's voice interrupts his childhood football thoughts. Jordan then opens the car door to enter their vehicle. Carter immediately follows suit as he enters the passenger side. Jordan starts the car and the detectives departs their current location.

Meanwhile, Jim Jordan was at home watching television to occupy his mind from Tina's death. He sat in his lazy-boy chair trying to erase her murder from his memory. Images of her brain matter splattered upon his chest kept playing over in his head. Jim eyes began to flutter as he gazed into space, letting the ambience of his television induce him into a twilight sleep. Jim began dreaming of making love to his late girlfriend. Jim loved Tina so much, but never told her how he really felt. The death of Kim kept his true feelings bottled inside. Suddenly, Jim's dream sequence began switching back and forth between the deaths of Tina and Kim. He began to whimper as each sequence played through his mind. Hours had passed through the night and Jim woke up crying for the two ladies he loved so dearly.

Wiping the tears from his eyes, Jim looked over at his cellphone and retrieved it from the coffee table. He then scrolled to his father's number and paused momentarily. Finally, Jim began dialing his father's number. Sergeant Jordan was sleeping on the sofa when his cellphone began vibrating on his chest. He wiped his eyes to focus on the incoming number and noticed it was Jim calling.

Jordan answered his phone with concern, "Are you ok son?"

Jim answered his father with a hesitant reply, "I, I have something to say."

"I'm listening son, go ahead." Jordan stated.

Jim's voice became crackled as he tried to explain his situation. Sergeant Jordan sat up to listen to what his son had to say. But Jim took his time to form the words he needed to speak. Sergeant Jordan scaled back the tone of his voice, giving assurance that everything will be okay.

"Go ahead son; tell me what's on your mind. I'm sure it can be worked out. I am here for whatever you may need," Jordan expressed.

"I am glad to know that. Because what I'm about to say will need your unconditional support and complete understanding." Jim stated.

"Jim, know that you're my son and I'm a dad first," said Jordan.

"I am a suspect in your murder investigation," exclaimed Jim.

Sergeant Jordan paused before responding to his son's comment. He then asked Jim his current location. Jim responded that he was at his apartment. Sergeant Jordan instructed his son to stay put and he would be there shortly. Jim terminated the call, waiting for his father's arrival.

CHAPTER FOUR: THE INTRODUCTION

It was an early morning before dawn; ODI Agents Tyler and Graham were on a surveillance detail, monitoring a semi-truck containing stolen merchandise. Intelligence lead them to believe the vehicle had been hi-jack by HHK, who was on payroll with Father Terry and his illicit business constituents. The two agents were positioned across the street in an unmarked vehicle, waiting to see who will retrieve the truck and its stolen contents.

"The sun will be up soon, what time is it?" Agent Tyler asked.

"4:30 a.m.!" Agent Graham replied.

The agents had been watching their target all night and into the morning. Intelligence listed the trailer to contain untaxed alcohol, which was stolen from the manufacturing company of Gordon's Cannery. Gordon's Cannery was owned by Ohio Liquor Commissioner, Constantine Gordon. He was also known as "Con-man Gordon," God-Nephew to the Late Lorenzo Oranthal and God-Brother to Terry Oranthal. Terry, also known as Father Terry, became a priest after being exiled from the mob. Everyone knew Gordon and Father Terry were at odds with each other. It was a miracle to see no bloodshed between the two since the death of the Don, Lorenzo Oranthal.

As time elapsed, the sun began illuminating the morning sky and revealing the agent's location. Just before their position was exposed, a green Chevy Nova approached the trucks location. The vehicle contained two occupants, in which the passenger of the vehicle exited and entered the trucks cabin.

"Heads up, we got bait," Agent Graham stated.

"It's about time. Let's see where these assholes are going." Agent Tyler responded.

The agent's intelligence informed them the truck may be driven to Cincinnati, Ohio to drop off its load. The green Nova and semi-truck left the surveyed location, tailed by the ODI agent's in a distant follow. As Agents Tyler and Graham continued their surveillance, they observed the two vehicles to take a truck route heading towards Interstate 271-South. The subject's maintained legal speed as to not alert attention to their illicit activity. Subsequently to the surveillance detail, Jordan's vehicle passes the agents as he heads to his son's apartment.

Moments later, Jordan arrives in front of building "D" of his son's apartment complex. Exiting his vehicle, Jordan enters the building and heads towards apartment "D-107." Jim's high-tech security system alerts him of his dad's arrival. Jim greets his dad with a brotherly hug. Jordan then walks into his son's apartment, discarding his shoes onto the runway mat. The two men sat at the dining table, Jim looking down at the table as his dad stared at him.

"Would you mind telling what's going on?" Jordan Asked.

Jim looks up and states, "You're going to find my DNA on Tina's body. We had sex!"

"Did you kill her?" Jordan asks.

"No, I loved her too much to do so. Pop, she was everything! We began dating two years ago with plans to marry in a few months. Due to you being a cop and her father having mob ties, we considered to keep our thing quiet until it was necessary. Pop, prior to her death, we had sex in the kitchen where you found her body. She and I stood before the kitchen window at the time of her death. We were making love by the kitchen window. I then heard the crackling of glass and felt her brains splatter onto my chest. Her body then fell upon the floor and I could see she wasn't moving. I looked out the broken window and saw a man with a rifle staged on the adjacent roof. He was about to take another shot, but I took cover on the floor. I didn't know what else to do. I then crawled to her   bedroom to retrieve my clothes. Getting out of there was the only thing on my mind!" Jim sadly explained.

"I want you to stay out of sight for a day or two. Your life may depend on it." Jordan instructed.

"For sure, anything you say pop," replied Jim.

Jordan then departed Jim's apartment and walked back to his car. He began reminiscing the night Kim was killed and identifying her body at the morgue. Jordan could vision the coroner pulling back the sheet which covered his daughter's body and as it unveiled, it was Jim's face he saw. He immediately felt his stomach drop as a nausea feeling came upon him. Jordan didn't want to lose another child to street violence. Therefore, his next move had to be calculated and impudent to the badge. Jordan starts his car and leaves the apartment complex.

Meanwhile at Detective Carter's apartment, he laid sleep dreaming of his days as a gang detective. Carter dreamt he was organizing a truce between gang members.   In his dream, Carter was speaking before a crowd of gang members from various sets. Carter's speech focused on creating a Community Retention and Intervention Plan; pledging to rebuild its neighborhoods. Suddenly in Carter's dream, a car drives onto their location and began shooting into the crowd. Carter's sees the passenger of the vehicle exits and began targeting specific gang members with his weapon. He further identifies the subject to display colors from the HHK (Harvard Heights Kings) gang set. Carter draws his weapon. A cloud of gun smoke blinds his sight of the shooter. As he fights through the smoke, a figure with shadowed features appears. Carter began shouting commands at the mysterious figure. The subject disappear as Carter is awakened by a vibrating noise. It was his cellphone ringing in current time.

"Hello," Carter answered in a tired voice.

It was Chief Jenkins, requesting a meeting with Carter and Jordan at their favorite Breakfast Diner. Carter was irritated by the phone call, but he knew not to refuse an invite from the Chief. Carter had to play politics, if he wanted to promote within the CPD. Jenkins advised him to alert Jordan and don't be late for the meeting. He then terminated the call, leaving Carter to carry out his instructions.

Sergeant Jordan was driving back to his residence when an unidentified vehicle turns out in front of him. The vehicle drives through a stop sign, causing Jordan to slam onto his brakes. Jordan activated his emergency lights to yield the vehicle to a stop. He then takes his badge from covered clothing and exits the vehicle. Jordan approaches the driver's vehicle with caution, slowly arriving to its driver-side window. The driver descends its window and displays a government badge.

"Who do you work for?" Jordan asks.

"Special Agent Raven Ford of ODI." The driver replied. Jordan adjusted his temperament after Agent Ford identified herself. He still counseled her for no regards of abiding the law. Ford smiled and apologized for her inadvertent actions. The counseling soon turns into a conversation of laughter, leading to the exchange of contact information.   Agent Ford drives off and Jordan begins thinking his new contact in law enforcement. Suddenly, his cellphone rings and its Carter calling him.

"Hey man, chief wants us to meet him at the Breakfast diner on Cedar and Lee Road." Carter advises.

Jordan frowns, because he knew he'd just left the area. He didn't feel like turning around, but he knew not to refuse an invite from the chief. Jordan advises Carter he would be there shortly.

"I hate playing politics." Jordan states as he gets into his vehicle and proceed to the dinner.
A few minutes down the road, Agent Ford receives a call from Agents Tyler and Graham. Her agents are tailing the semi-truck with stolen alcohol. As Agent Tyler reports in current time regarding their surveillance, they encounter a black Dodge Charger with smoked tint windows. The Charger side-strikes the agent's vehicle, causing Agent Tyler to over-correct his steering and evade crashing into another vehicle.   Agent Graham retrieves his weapon from a shoulder holster.

"What's going on?" Ford asked.

"We've been sideswiped by an identified vehicle. Wait, hold on. It looks like they are trying to knock us off the road." Tyler exclaims.

"Gun, gun, backseat passenger has a gun!" Agent Graham shouted.

The driver of the black Charger tries to parallel his vehicle with the agent's vehicles. Agent Ford began to hear the exchange of gun fire over her cellphone. At this time, she radioed for assisting law enforcement units to aid her agents.

"What is your location?" Ford asked.

"71-Southbound by Mile Marker-72, just outside the City of Akron!" Tyler shouted.

Agent Ford could hear distress in Tyler's voice as sounds of gunfire rang out from her cellphone.

"I'm down to my last magazine, where the fuck is our back up?" Graham shouted.

  Seconds seemed like minutes during the horrific exchange of gunfire. Agent Tyler accelerated their vehicle to escape the oncoming bullets, but the Charger immediately closes their gap. Traveling at speeds close to 95-miles per hour and now parallel of one another, the Charger's driver-side window descends. Its driver extends a sawed-off shotgun outside the window and discharges four rounds into the passenger side of the Agents vehicle. Tyler manages to steer their vehicle onto the grassy median, but only after Agent Graham is fatally struck by shotgun rounds. The black Charger and the stolen truck of liquor continues its travel on 71-Southbound.   Distant sounds of police sirens became louder as Tyler held his partner's lifeless body in his arms. Tyler lets out a battle cry as tears fell from his eyes.

It's 10:30 a.m. on the northeast side of Cleveland; Sergeant Jordan is meeting with Detective Carter and Chief Jenkins. Jordan enters the "Breakfast Diner" and locates his colleagues at a secluded booth. Carter breaks conversation with the Chief and waves Jordan over to their table. Jordan walks over and greets them both as he sits down.

"Glad you gentlemen could make it," express the Chief.

"As if we had a choice, but I am sure there's a good reason for this." Jordan stated.

"Your assumptions are right." Jenkins chuckled in his reply.

Jenkins continued speaking on how he felt Lopez' murder investigation and Gordon Cannery may be related. Carter supported the Chief's theory by advising on how Lopez was the daughter of Ohio Liquor Commissioner, Constantine Gordon. He further stated Lopez didn't want to carry her father's name due to his political and mob affiliations. Carter believed someone found out the connection and killed Lopez to hurt her father. Jenkins concurred with Carter's comment, suggesting it was more about the business operations of Gordon Cannery.

The Chief's assumption about Gordon Cannery was correct. Unknown to the three lawmen, Gordon Cannery was the largest manufacturer in the northeast region. Its distribution authority covered cities of the Midwest onto eastern states. Authority of this magnitude would allow other illicit activities to incur without notice. The missing part of Lopez' murder was the "who." Who would go to measures of murder to derail the lucrative business of Gordon Cannery? The lawmen knew Gordon's political career alone, enlisted multiple suspects as well as his mob ties.

"Chief, why are we meeting here instead of your office? You think your office is bugged?" Carter asked.

Jenkins smiled, followed by a soft chuckle and said, "No you fart nugget, I was hungry and thought to buy you two mopes some breakfast."

Back at the death scene of Agent Mookie Graham, Agent Ford arrives to speak with local authorities and debrief with Agent Tyler. Tyler had remnants of brain matter upon his right shoulder and face area. Ford look over towards the agent's vehicle. She could see Graham's body still in the passenger seat. She walked over for a closer examination and observed Graham's face to be partially disfigured from shotgun pellets.

"What the fuck happened?" Ford shouted.

She began to whimper, but the adrenalin compelled her from breaking down before her law enforcement peers. Agent Ford wanted real time intelligence on Graham's murder, and she wanted it sooner than later.   She instructed Tyler to seek medical treatment while waiting for Agents Duncan and Stanzell to arrive. Ford then got into her vehicle and departed the scene with intentions of following up on some leads.

On the southeast side of Cleveland in vicinity of Garfield Heights, Father Terry was conducting a christening at Saint Terry's Catholic Church. The inaugural ceremony was also a cover meeting with one of Terry's illicit constituents. Concluding the sacred baptism, Father Terry met with HHK Lieutenant, Jaden Kraus. Jaden was son of former CPD Detective, Mark Kraus.

"I heard there was an incident on I-71 south today." Father Terry stated.

"There was, but it didn't stop the ordered business at hand. The shipment made it to its destination on time. All revenue from our shipment will be washed through my father's business." Jaden replied.

Jaden and Terry were meeting in a confession booth as they conducted business. Father Terry then inquired about the ongoing homicide Investigation at Kraus's, regarding HHK member "Shorty". Jaden assured Father Terry the ongoing investigation wouldn't interfere with their business as well. He made reference that an inside man at CPD would dissolve the open murder into a cold case.   Shortly after their conversation, Jaden exited the confession booth and Father Terry remained inside. Terry was reflecting upon the events which occurred earlier on I-71 southbound. He knew the death of a State Agent would bring the over watch of ODI.

Currently at the apartment of Jim Jordan, sounds of running water escapes a misty bathroom. Suddenly the water stops and Jim exits with a towel around his waist. He then walks into his bedroom and turns on the television. The volume is low as he watches live video coverage of a crime scene. The headline posted across the screen reads "Law Enforcement official killed in the line of duty". Jim reaches for his TV remote and turns up the volume. The voice of a female reporter indicates a government agent was murdered on I-71 southbound, just outside the city limits of Akron.

Jim observed emergency medical personnel removing a covered body from a vehicle and placing it onto a gurney. WCJC-Channel 18 news had no information on the decease's identity. Concern of Akron City limits being adjacent to Cleveland's, Jim contacted his father's cellphone. Seconds later, Sergeant Jordan answered his phone. Jim became immediately relieved upon hearing his father's voice.

Sergeant Jordan assured his son he was fine and after a short conversation between the two, Jim told his father they would speak later. The phone call ended with Jordan pondering the inquiry of the dead officer's identity. He then conferred with Carter and the Chief about his call. Chief Jenkins immediately called his confidential contacts and learns it was an ODI Agent killed in the line of duty. The three lawmen ordered drinks in honor of a fallen colleague.

CHAPTER FIVE: THE OFFER

It's the fall of 1992 and night has fallen upon the City of Baghdad. Scud missiles scour the night skies in prevent of an air assault from enemy forces. Below this adversity, a dense smell of cordite engulfs the night air as ground troops are encountering high interest targets.

Among the distinct personnel of military forces is an elite group identified as SEAL Team 5. The strategic group of soldiers is led by Lieutenant Terrence Tyler. As Tyler and his men move from cover to cover, the ground around them shook from contact of exploding ordnance devices.

LT. Tyler orders his team to cease movement to evade the debris of ricocheting bullets. The unit embarked themselves in a nearby trench for cover. Tyler calls a scout to his location. Warrant Officer James arrived to take his orders. Tyler instruct the newly and young member of their unit to map a safe route out of gunfire. The young officer accepts his orders and set out to find a safe path. As he moves through open terrain, the soldier is struck down by a sniper's bullet.

Agent Tyler wakes out of his dream and sits up in the bed. He has stammering breathing and his hands are shaking. Tyler reaches for a bottle of water sitting on his night stand and began taking big gulps. He then throws an empty bottle onto the floor after consuming its contents.

Looking around the bedroom and trying to gather his bearings, Tyler focuses upon the clock sitting on the night stand. Its 9:00 am, two hours before Agent Graham's funeral services. Tyler rises from his bed and enters the bathroom to shower.

Birds are chirping freely on a fall morning as sunlight glitters through tree leaves. The Jordan's are standing before Kim's headstone at Calvary Cemetery. Mrs. Jordan whispers an indistinctive prayer for her daughter, while Jim and Sergeant Jordan stands by her side.

"I miss you sis," Jim whispers as a single tear rolled down his right cheek.

Mrs. Jordan looks over at her son, cuddles his cheek with a single hand and smooths away his tear. She then kisses the opposite cheek and whispers, "she misses you too. "

Currently on the other side of Calvary Cemetery at 11:05 a.m., fellow agents and friends attend the outdoor funeral services of Agent Graham. Pastor John of Canaan Catholic Church gives the eulogy of the fallen hero. Agents Ford, Tyler, Stanzell and Duncan show primary presence for their lost brother.

The prestige Pastor of Cleveland begins to speak in high regards of Agent Mookiah "Mookie" Graham. He describes him as a pillar of the Greater Cleveland area. Pastor John indicated how his family has suffered from a legacy of deaths, losing his father to a fatal shooting by overzealous police and his brother to suicide.

Suddenly, the voice of Pastor John became inaudible upon the ears of Mrs. Graham. She began reminiscing the night her husband was murdered by racist's policemen. In spite of the disheartening details, Mookie became a law enforcement agent to deter the injustice of blind justice. Knowing that all law enforcement officials were not the same as those he'd encountered growing up, allowed him to become a "Black Shield" of his community. The pastor's voice became audible again as Mrs. Graham transition her focus back into the present.

"From clay you were made and as ashes you will return. May your spirit rise to the lord in heaven. For your soul is his to keep. In the name of the father, his son and our Holy Spirit, Amen." Pastor John prayed, illustrating the sign of a cross upon his chest.

The attending guest began placing roses onto Mookie's coffin. Agent Ford started to cry as Graham's coffin was lowered into the ground. She then regroups and gathers her emotions as her team steps in to console her.

"I vow, we will vow, to get the bastardized group responsible for this." Agent Tyler whispers in Ford's ear.

Ford wipes away her tears and retrieves a cellphone from inside her coat. She then dials the numbers to Sergeant Jordan's phone. Seconds later, a vibrating noise comes from inside Sergeant Jordan's jacket. He retrieved his cellphone to answer a call.

"Hello, who's this?" Jordan answered.

"We have to meet, where are you?"   Ford asked.

Jordan advised Agent Ford he was at Calvary Cemetery. Ford then told him she was there too. The two agree to meet at a nearby median point for convenience.
Mrs. Jordan questioned her husband about his call which interfered with their family time. Sergeant Jordan explained it was work and he had to meet a contact nearby in the cemetery. Not happy with the interruption, Mrs. Jordan understood it had to be important for the sergeant to leave their side. Jim assures his dad he would get his mom home safe. Kissing his wife and giving his son a hug, Jordan left to meet with Agent Ford.

As planned, Sergeant Jordan and Agent Ford met at a point of the cemetery. Their location landed them inside a desolated shed near the southeast entrance.

"Interesting place to meet," chuckled Jordan.

 Agent Ford advised she'd conducted many covert meetings in the cemetery shed. Ford then hands Jordan a large envelope containing photos of him in various places. He looked at her with concerns of why she had these photos.

"Yes, I've been surveilling you for weeks. It wasn't by coincidence you pulled my vehicle over. I planned that incident, to meet you of course and know my recruit." Ford stated.

Jordan was even more confused of why Agent Ford was trying to recruit him. Although he has interests of becoming an ODI Agent, Jordan didn't think he was a favorable recruit. Ford explained to Jordan, he was a natural at what he does as a cop. She knew his transition to an agent would be easy. Ford informed Jordan she had an open spot in her unit. Jordan eyes widen with surprise.

"Just like that I'm in your unit?" Jordan asked.

Agent Ford Chuckled As she responded to Jordan's question. "I will bring you on as a liaison agent. Give you a taste of what is expected and further examine your skill as to see if you're a true fit. We can fast track your application as a formality while you are a liaison, should I choose to keep you."

Sergeant Jordan smiles at the offer. He promises to get back with Ford regarding his answer. She advises Jordan not to take her offer unlikely. Ford further instructed him there was a 72-hour window for a decision to be made. The two law enforcement officials departed with intent to speak on a later date.

"Remember, 72-hours. Tick-tock, tick-tock!" Agent Ford commented upon her departure.

A day later, Jordan was sitting at his desk completing an overdue report for the Chief. Indistinctive chatter along with ringing phones, ambience the duty room of the Hazardous Targets Section. Suddenly, Jordan stopped typing and looked around the office. He noticed Detective Carter was nowhere to be found. It was 9:30 a.m. and Carter was an hour late for work. Jordan's desk phone began ringing with the Chiefs extension on display. He was hesitant to answer, but he didn't want to delay the inevitable.

"Hello, yes Sir. I'm on my way." Jordan stated.

Jordan gathered his report and left to meet with the Chief. He entered the elevator car adjacent from the HTS office. As the doors drew together, a pasty hand breaches and prevents them from closing. Peering into the elevator was a familiar face.

"Good morning partner," Detective Carter greets Jordan with a smirking grin.

"It's about time you showed up." Jordan replied.

Carter chuckled and replied to Jordan's comment. "I've been here, reviewing forensics from the Lopez' murder."

Jordan eyes widen from Carter's comment. He became worried about the mentioned results. Discreetly, Jordan tries to pick Carter's brain for intel of what he knew. Carter uttered cynical remarks to keep Jordan wondering as to play a "Cat and Mouse" game of entertainment. Jordan's face showed dislike to Carter's attempt to be amusing. The elevator doors open and Jordan exit displaying his left middle-finger to Carter's face. Carter chuckles as the two detectives walks into the Chief's office.

10 a.m., reads a clock on the wall inside a neighborhood coffee shop. Jim sat reading an article from the Cleveland Press newspaper. The article read about the death of Mookiah Graham and his contributions to the Greater Cleveland Area. It further read he was being named as the city's black shield of his community. Counter comments protested the idea, indicating it would segregate law enforcement officers in the community. Jim scoffed at the counter comments. He remembered the childhood incident which changed Agent Graham's life forever. Graham's father was killed the same week Jim lost his sister. The two incidents made big news in the black communities of Cleveland, signifying a common denominator to police involved shootings.

Jim took a final sip of his beverage and gets up to leaves the coffee shop. He notices a black Charger idling in a marked parking space. The vehicle was facing Jim's direction as he exits the establishment. Jim discretely looks over his left shoulder and noticed the vehicle backing out from its parked position. He made a quick right as to see if the vehicle would trail his steps. Jim took refuge behind a nearby trash dumpster, waiting to see if the vehicle would appear.

The vehicle appeared seconds later and idled for five minutes. It was obvious occupants inside the vehicle were trying to locate Jim. Unable to locate him, the black Charger leaves the parking lot with screeching tires. Observing the vehicle's departure, Jim left his concealed location in route to his vehicle. Feeling paranoid of being followed, Jim took an evasive route to his apartment as a precaution.

Meanwhile at CPD Headquarters, Detective Carter was debriefing Jordan and Chief Jenkins. The forensic report revealed fluids found on Lopez' body was semen and not vaginal discharge. Carter indicated of processing the results through COTAS, but was unable to find a match.

He made sure the DNA results were saved in COTAS for future matches. Jordan was relieved the report didn't indicate his son as a suspect, but concerned his son's DNA was now in a police data base. Jordan knew time would later be an enemy of his son's fate. The semen found on Lopez' body could very well witness Jim as a suspect. Chief Jenkins was happy with Carter's results. He even gave him indefinite resources to conclude his findings.

"It seems you all have it handle here." Jordan stated as he attempted to leave.

"Not so fast Sergeant. I'm going to need your back channel resources to cut some red tape. Commissioner Gordan is playing hardball in cooperating with our investigation. You think your connection with the Governor's office may be of some help?" Jenkins inquired.

"Sure Chief, I look into it for you. If you don't mind, I have something to check on and then I'll follow up with my contact." Jordan stated.

"No worries, we can catch up later!" Jenkins replies.

Forty-five miles northeast of Cleveland in the City of Youngstown, Agent Stanzell was having a sit down with Michael Calzoni. Calzoni was the newly name Don of the Cleveland mafia. Stanzell and Calzoni played on the same high school football team at Youngstown Mooney. The two reminisced about the old days for a moment and then Stanzell stated his real reason for their reunion.

"It's been a while bro, what's good?" Calzoni greeted.

"You remember Mookie Graham, right? He was St. Peter Chanel's star receiver back in the day. Well, his funeral was yesterday." Stanzell replied.

Calzoni's eyes widen with surprise as he displayed concern for a fellow athlete. Stanzell informed his former teammate of Graham being an ODI agent killed in the line of duty.

"How did he die?" Calzoni asks.

Stanzell explained Agent Graham was killed from a Shotgun blast to the chest, while he and another agent were surveilling a stolen liquor truck. Stanzell then asked Calzoni did he know anything about the heist. Calzoni told his old friend the truck belonged to Gordon Cannery, but he wasn't sure who was behind the heist or who killed his colleague. Calzoni promised to listen out for any leads to catching those responsible for Graham's death. Agent Stanzell gave Calzoni a fist bump and told him to keep in touch. Just as Stanzell is about to leave, Calzoni poses question to his former teammate.

"Why didn't you come work for the family, cousin?" Calzoni asks.

Stanzell smiles and replies, "Someone has to keep you out of prison, cousin!"

Nine hours later, Mirage on The Water was hosting their "Jeans and Moët" gala. ODI Agents were onsite working an undercover prostitution and narcotics ring. Agent Duncan was lead investigator, while being supported by Agents Stanzell and Tyler. Duncan with the assistance of her confidential informant (CI) sat at the main bar of the nightclub. The bartender approaches Duncan and her CI to take their drink orders. Duncan orders two Vodka-Cranberries.

"That's usually a man's drink or a woman making a statement," commented the bartender.

"It's been a long week, not mentioning today's list of bullshit. My girl and I just want to unwind."   Duncan replied.

The bartender smiled and left to retrieve their orders. Agents Stanzell and Tyler were posted in the VIP section overlooking the main bar area. Tyler was enjoying the scenery of half-naked females wearing "below the vagina" miniskirts. A waitress walks over to their location and asks to take their drink order.

"What can I get you boys?" The waitress asked.

"Let me have a double Scotch on the rocks. My light skinned brother will have a double Vodka on the rocks." Tyler replied.

The waitress looks over at Stanzell, biting her bottom lip and giving him an inviting look of sex. Stanzell intentionally ignores the waitress' gesture. Tyler lights a cigar and sits back to observe the obvious attraction by the waitress. After several seconds of intense staring, Tyler Clears his throat to regain waitress' attention.

"Snowflake, you want to get those drinks?" Tyler asks.

The waitress looks back at Tyler, smiled and walks away to retrieve their drinks. Tyler began shaking his head in disbelief of the affect Stanzell have on women. Stanzell sucks his teeth and looks over at Tyler with a confident stare.

Currently at the main bar, the bartender returned with drinks for Duncan and her CI. Duncan takes a sip of her beverage and nods in agreement to its taste. She then licks her lips as a seductive gesture towards the bartender. The bartender smiles in appreciation of his services.

"Not bad, not bad at all. What else are you good at?" Duncan asks.

"What do you have a taste for?" The bartender responds as he raises an eyebrow in curiosity.

Agent Duncan smiled and replies, "I have a diverse taste for an explicit menu."

The bartender nodded in agreement and asks, "A la carte or combo?"

"I'm usually a la carte girl but will be open to a combo selection." Duncan stated.

"Let me see what I can do." The bartender replies.

Meanwhile in the VIP section, Tyler and Stanzell keeps over watch. Tyler was getting excited about all the pretty women in the club. Stanzell reminded him to stay focus on their operation. He then gets up to use the restroom.
"I'll be back, have to take a piss!" Stanzell stated.

Stanzell walks towards the restroom area, where he comes upon a unisex restroom between the men's and women's restroom area. He enters the unisex restroom but forgets to lock the door behind him. Seconds after his entry, the flirtatious waitress walks in unannounced. Stanzell turns around with his zipper undone. The waitress exposes his penis and began performing fellatio on him. After a few minutes goes by, Stanzell takes his penis out of the waitress' mouth. She then stands up and he positions her over the toilet. He then inserts his penis inside her from behind.

Agent Duncan transmits across her hidden radio. "You guys copy me? I may have a buy with the bartender."

Agent Tyler acknowledged Duncan's radio communication. He then messaged Stanzell by text, "where are you? Duncan is about to make a move. Hurry back!"

Minutes later, Stanzell arrives back to the VIP section. Seconds after his arrival, the flirtatious waitress brings their drinks and a napkin with her number on it. Tyler looked at the waitress and then over at Stanzell. He noticed his partner to have a mischievous look upon his face.

"Tell me you didn't tap that?" Tyler asked.

Agent Stanzell gave a sly smile while downing the last contents of his drink. Tyler shook his head as he and Stanzell left their seating area to assist Duncan. Tyler looked back at their table and observed the waitress preparing it for the next patron.

"I guess no tip is needed since you already tipped her. You know, you're something else and has the nerve to tell me stay focus." Tyler stated.

Agent Duncan and her CI were making their way to the patio of the night club; Agents Tyler and Stanzell weren't too far behind. Out of nowhere the bartender appeared with a gun concealed under a white towel. The possessed weapon was a Glock-26 with a silencer attached.

"Do as I say, and I won't have to shoot your black ass." The bartender stated.

Agent Duncan didn't want to escalate the situation and cause an innocent bystander to be hurt. As they made their way to an adjacent boating dock, Duncan tried to distract the assailant with sexual overtones. Her CI picked up on the charades and joined in. The CI turned to the assailant and uncovered her breast. The sexual gesture was enough to bring him to a halt, giving Agents Tyler and Stanzell time to jump his position. The agents rendered the bartender unconscious and placed him onto a boat operated by Agent Ford.

"Good work team. Now let's see what he knows." Ford stated.

A half an hour later, the bartender awakens in bondage below the deck of Agent Ford's boat. Ford steered the boat about a mile offshore for privacy during their interrogation of the bartender. Thirty minutes into an intense interview led by Tyler, the agents learned liquid cocaine was being transported in liquor bottles to major nightclubs throughout the city. Interested parties would dehydrate the cocaine back into a powder form and packaged for distribution.

"Who are these interested parties," asked Stanzell.

The bartender stated he didn't know. He just ran the prostitution side of things.
Ford and her agents agreed a prostitution bust was only peanuts compared to the narcotics distribution. Holding the crime of attempt murder over the bartender's head, Agent Ford decided to enlist him as an undocumented CI. However, Agent Tyler promised to kill the bartender should he foil their investigation. The agents returned the bartender to the boating docks, advising he would be contacted at a later date. Ford gave him a burner cellphone for future contact.

Currently uptown at Kraus' Gentlemen's Club, Father Terry was meeting with Kraus himself. The two men were discussing illicit business for their next criminal enterprise. Terry kept his distance with everyone whom he conducted business with. He was one to never trust anyone but keep everyone confused and guessing. Kraus on the other hand loved money and only saw the color of green when conducting business.

"The liquor you heisted came in handy. I was able to restock my bottles without any overhead. Just like the old prohibition days." Kraus Stated.

Father Terry replies with a condescending remark, "You mean the alcohol your son stole for me. He's a good little soldier who knows his place."

Kraus scoffs at Terry's remark and rebuttal, "Don't let that white collar around your neck give you false confidence. Money from my illegal gambling and prostitution is washed through your congregation's money. Don't forget that my friend."

After Kraus reminds Terry of his place in their relationship, Father Terry downs a double shot of Jamison and walks out the back entrance of the establishment. Kraus could do nothing but laugh at the reaction displayed on Terry's face. On the other hand, Kraus didn't like the idea of his son doing Terry's bidding either. For he knew it would only be a matter of time before Jaden becomes Terry's patsy.

The digital clock on Jim's night stand reads 1:15 a.m. He's currently sleeping in his bed until the sounds of crushed glass echoes in his apartment. Previously before going to bed, Jim placed a sandwich bag of crushed glass under his floor mat and created a homemade alarm. The intruder stepped on it, alerting Jim out of his sleep. Foreign to the apartment's diagram, the intruder could only assume Jim's location in the apartment. Seconds became minutes and minutes felt like a lonely hour of the intruder's desolate search for Jim. Upon reaching the threshold of Jim's bedroom, the assailant trained his weapon onto Jim's bed, confirming a target to engage. Before discharging his weapon, the intruder heard words of an unfavorable outcome to his disadvantaged position.

"Looking for me?" Jim asked the assailant before shooting him dead.

An hour later, CPD Officers are investigating a shooting at Jim's apartment. As the Coroner secures the decease in a body bag, Sargent Jordan arrives on scene. He's briefed by the primary officer in charge and learns the decease is a CPD officer. Unclear of the evidentiary circumstances, Jim is placed into custody and transported to CPD headquarters.

Later that morning around 9:30 a.m., Sergeant Jordan and his wife are discussing the events leading up to their son's arrest. Jordan tries to console his wife in the event of easing her worries about Jim. He tells her he has a plan and a friend who could help. Mrs. Jordan questioned her husband as to whom could help with her son's situation. Jordan looks at his watch and observes he has three hours to submit his answer to Agent Ford. He takes out his phone to contact her.

"What are you doing?" Pam asks.

"Calling in a favor and making a commitment." Jordan stated.

The phone of Agent Ford's vibrates across her nightstand. She's awakens by the thudding sound and slow to answer its call. "This is Ford," answering in a tired voice.

Jordan's voice comes across her phone, alerting they needed to meet. He advises for a rendezvous at Lancers for an early brunch. Three hours later at 12:30pm, Agent Ford and Sergeant Jordan meets for brunch. He advises his son is in CPD custody for killing an off-duty officer. Jordan continued to state that the officer broke into his son's home.

"What was the officer's name," asked Agent Ford.

Jordan identified the officer as Patrolman Atkins. Agent Ford informed him the decease had associations with HHK. She further indicated Atkins as a suspect in the Lopez's murder. The new information enticed Jordan's decision to accept Agent Ford's offer. Concluding Jordan's commitment, Ford promised to help Jordan's son.

3:00 pm at CPD Headquarters, Sergeant Jordan's son is being prepared for transport to Garfield Police Department (GPD). Chief Jenkins authorized covert custody to protect Jim while being processed through the system. Agent Ford and her team was in the vicinity conducting surveillance on the transport. As the transport van departs CPD Sally Port, ODI Agents followed in a near distant.

3:45 pm, CPD transport van arrives at GPD sally port. Officer's handpicked by Chief Jenkins exchange custody of Jim Jordan with GPD Officers. He's then taking to a private room, off books of general population. 4:15 pm, Agent Duncan appears as counsel for Jim Jordan. She meets with him in the private room.

"Who are you?" Jim asks.

"I'm your counsel and a friend of your pops. Keep your mouth shut and do as I say. You'll be out of here soon." Duncan instructed.

Jim didn't question Duncan instruction. She advised Jim they would be before a judge in fifteen minutes. Duncan told Jim she would do all the talking and speak only when instructed too. Jim agreed with no intent to foil his chances of being released.

4:45 pm, Jim and Agent Duncan appears before a judge along with a Special Prosecutor. The prosecutor stands before the judge to present his case against Jim.   Jim sat adjacent the prosecutor's table and listens to the infractions read against him.

"Your honor, the state submits charges of manslaughter in the second degree upon the defendant." Prosecutor stated.

Jim frowns after hearing the charges and wants to give his opinion, but he remembers what Agent Duncan said. He looked onto her for permission to speak, but she spoke instead. Agent Duncan stands before the judge after the State present their charges.

"Your honor, my client pleads not guilty. I further requests bail for his release!" Duncan request.

The Special Prosecutor did not oppose and just like that, Jim was released from custody. Agent Duncan whispers into Jim's ear, giving him instructions to look for Agent Tyler upon exiting the courtroom. She described Tyler to be wearing a FUBU sweat suit, black in color with blue trim. Jim exist the courtroom and meets up with Tyler.

"I'm Agent Tyler, here on behalf of your father. Let's move!"

Jim and Agent Tyler exited the courthouse, later entering a black Dodge Intrepid. Tyler then drives Jim to Calvary Cemetery, where he meets his dad and Agent Ford. Jim, his dad and Agent Ford are standing before Kim's headstone.

"Dad, what are we doing here," asked Jim.

"Protecting you, and allowing you to have a future," replied Sergeant Jordan.

Agent Ford interrupts their conversation. She explains to Jim, the deceased CPD officer was also an associate of HHK. Agent Ford further implicated HHK to be working with Father Terry. She went on to tell Jim, he could only say his goodbyes for now and later return once things die down. Jim did just that, said his goodbyes to his father, mother and Kim. Mrs. Jordan tells her son goodbye through FaceTime call. Jim eyes began tearing as he observed his mother's tears. Sergeant Jordan tells his son they have to leave. He then drives him to the U.S. Coast Guard base in Maumee, just outside Toledo, OH. The two men say their temporary goodbyes, but look to see each other soon.

CHAPTER SIX: TRAINING DAY (PART 1)

Three weeks later at an undisclosed training facility for ODI Agents, gunfire echoes across an open field. Agents Stanzell, Tyler and Duncan are conducting their quarterly weapons qualification. Agent Ford walks onto the outdoor shooting range with Sergeant Jordan and introduces him to the team.

"Say hello to our newest member, Sergeant Jordan. He will be joining our unit as a liaison Agent". Ford introduced.

Ford then walks Jordan over to a table of weapons. She begins his introduction to training with the expectations of Jordan becoming an ODI Agent. Ford explained all ODI agents will be proficient with multiple weapons. She indicated no agent will be deficient in their duties while assigned to her team. Ford then gave Jordan a MP5 to start his training. Jordan spent the next eight hours of his day training on multiple weapons and going through Practical Assimilation Training, known as PAT's. PAT's was created to give officers real live training scenarios to prevent fault when discharging their duties.

The next day, Jordan and his new team of colleagues are investigating a homicide related to mafia activity. Sonny "Fats" Gillespie had been bondage and beaten in his luxurious home located in Bratenahl, Ohio. The County Coroner estimated he'd been dead for at least eight days due to his decomposed body. Agents could barely speak without gagging or expelling their stomach fluids. Gillespie's eyes were cauterized, signifying he'd seen something he wasn't supposed to. The coroner suspected the victim's eyes were burn by a Taser and advised to know more after the autopsy.

Later that day, Agent Ford met with a Federal Prosecutor at the Cleveland Field Office of ODI. Ford was inquiring about clues to assist with the Gillespie homicide. Assistant U.S. Attorney Rowen indicated Gillespie was under federal surveillance pending transfer into witness protection. The government wanted his testimony against Ohio Liquor

Commissioner, Constantine Gordon. Commissioner Gordon was on the government's radar for racketeering and other organized crime activities.

"May I speak to your surveillance team assigned to Gillespie?" Agent Ford asked.

Prosecutor Rowen agreed to the request, but instructed Ford to tread lightly in questioning. He then arranged for a meeting at the Northern District of Ohio, U.S. Attorney Office. Ford agreed to the wishes of the AUSA and later scheduled her visit with his surveillance team.

Currently at CPD headquarters, Carter is corroborating facts relevant to his murder case. Chief Jenkins walks into the HTS Office and sees Carter typing away at his desk. The officer's immediately stood attention as the Chief entered the room. Everyone except Carter noticed the Chief's presence.

"At ease gentlemen," stated Chief Jenkins.

The Chief walks over to Carter's desk as everyone else returns back to their duties. He noticed Carter to have a small set of headphones in his ears. Carter was listening to a taped interrogation of a suspect. He then noticed the Chief standing before him and immediately stood at attention. Jenkins chuckled and told him to relax. He then told Carter he will be working the Lopez murder alone.

Carter scoffs at the news and then asked, "what about Jordan?"

Jenkins told Carter he'd been reassigned to work a joint investigation and to mind his business by focusing on the Lopez murder. Carter didn't like the idea of being shut out on anything. He was curious of what Jordan was involved with and whom.

Currently during confessions at Father Terry's church, Jaden meets with Father Terry in a confession booth. Terry's not happy about Atkins being killed in the residence of Jim Jordan. Jaden was surprise of how fast Father Terry found out about Atkins' death.

"You don't miss a beat." Jaden stated.

Father Terry scoffs at Jaden's remark and counsels him to clean up his act. Jaden took Father Terry's advice to be clear and concise. He knew further mishaps would bring substantial consequences.

"I wish no disrespect sir. I'll make sure his death doesn't lead back to our operation." Jaden advised.

Father Terry took Jaden statement as assurance to rectify any incursions of their illicit operations. Jaden departs Farther Terry with blessings of new opportunities. While exiting the church and later entering his vehicle, Jaden retrieves a burner cellphone from his glove compartment. He dials unknown digits of an influential character. After three rings, a voice comes across Jaden phone. Jaden acknowledges the voice and advise they must meet.

Brisk rain falls against the block windows of the County morgue, followed by a freezer door unlatching. The medical examiner retrieves Gillespie body from inside. He then transports it onto the autopsy table. As the medical examiner begins his preliminary examination, Agent Tyler and liaison Agent Jordan walks in.

"What do you have doc?" Tyler asks.

"I have nothing at the moment! I'm just about to start," replied the examiner.

He continues his examination, searching for trace evidence to conclude the manner of death. After cutting open the decease and removing Gillespie body organs, the medical examiner confirmed he died of cardiac arrest. The C.O.D was related to extensive Voltage from a Taser gun over an extended amount of time.

"Now that we know how this fat-fuck died, let's find out why." Agent Tyler stated.

The Agents noted their findings and left the morgue to build a case. Jordan being new to the team followed the lead of his senior, Agent Tyler. Although Tyler was lead agent, Jordan still had his reservations about the murder.

Two and a half hours south of Cleveland and in the City of Reynoldsburg, Jaden Kraus is meeting Commissioner Gordon at De Sal's Catholic Church. The two men sat six pews away from the alter as they conversated.

"You have a Lot of balls calling me. Ghost contact only!" · Gordon stated.

Jaden sucks his teeth before responding to Gordon's comment. "I wanted to see your face, when I told you that your associate who saw evil is now speaking no evil. You should know he's on a slab at the county morgue."

Commissioner Gordon chuckled, "I appreciate what you did or did not do. Your action will not go unnoticed."

Jaden scoffed and commented to have nothing to do with Gillespie's death, but indicated Father Terry May be involved.

"You expect me to believe that Judas-Priest killed Fats Gillespie? He never had the balls to do his own work. Terry always found a flunky to do his bidding. I hope you're not freelancing for him." Gordon stated.

Jaden denied any involvement with Father Terry, only pledging allegiance to himself. He advised the commissioner of being a friend should he ever need one. Gordon smiles in agreement to the offer. Jaden rises from his seat and exits the church. Gordon stays behind to give thanks for his daily blessings.

Jaden's trip to Reynoldsburg took him two and a half hours out of Cleveland. He decided to drive into Columbus and meet an old flame at the University. Jaden arrived at Jennings Hall, apartment living for graduate students not living in dorms. He enters the complex and knocks on the door of apartment #108. The door opens and a light-skinned woman with green eyes stand before Jaden in a cloth robe.

"What's up Carmella." Jaden greeted.

Inviting Jaden into her apartment, Carmella greets him with a kiss and states, "It's been a while and a girl has needs you know."

Jaden smiles at Carmella's comment. He then opens her robe, baring her naked body underneath. Jaden gently tilts Carmella head to his left and began kissing her neck. His kisses traveled slowly towards her breasts, causing each nipple to erect. Carmella moans as Jaden began sucking her breasts. He then lifts her off the floor and lays Carmella upon the kitchen island. With her legs open, Jaden began kisses and lick her vagina. Minutes goes by, Carmella's body began to convulse as the sounds of her moans become intense. Jaden smiles, knowing she's on the verge to cum. Just before she can climax, he inserts himself inside of her. The sounds of wet sex echoes in the kitchen, indicating a strong connection between the two.

Somewhere in the nightclub of "Vel's on The Circle", Agent Tyler is trailing a high valued target through a back hallway of the club. The target leads Tyler to the main kitchen area where he's met by two other subjects. Outnumbered three to one, Tyler had to rely on his military training. He engaged the subjects in a fisticuff, using martial art and grappling fighting techniques. As the subjects seem to get the best of Agent Tyler, Liaison Agent Jordan arrive just in time to assist his partner. The two agents rendered the subjects unconscious. Tyler began to search the subdued subjects for intelligence purposes. He found an encrypted MP3 player. Tyler secures the device and radios to Agent Ford, advising their possession. Ford acknowledges, informing them to meet her and Duncan at a nearby parking lot. As Tyler and Jordan exists the club, Agent Stanzell pulls up to retrieve them in a dark sedan. Jordan and Tyler moved quickly as to not be noticed during their departure.

Minutes later, the agents met up to debrief on their newly found evidence. Duncan informs her team that the device Agents Tyler and Jordan found has shipping dates for incoming narcotics.

"How do you know of this information?" Stanzell asks.

"My CI who accompanied me at the Mirage the other night, informed me. That's why Tyler and Jordan were in recon of our high valued targets." Duncan stated.

Although the agents had the shipping and distribution manifest, they still needed to decrypt the device. Jordan mentioned to have a contact in CPD's IT support. Agent Ford agreed on outsourcing assistance to decrypt the device. Jordan takes out his cell and dials the number to his IT friend.

"Hello, Korda, this is Jordan. Brother, I need your assistance on an off-book assignment. I can meet you at CPD headquarters tomorrow. Ok thanks, I'll be in touch."

Jordan's contact agreed to help, putting the agents closer to solving their narcotics case. Ford liked that Jordan was becoming resourceful in his early stages as an agent. The team broke location and agreed to meet once Jordan had more intelligence on the device.

Meanwhile at Carmella's apartment, she and Jaden lay sleeping in bed. The vibrating sounds of Jaden's cellphone awakens him. He answers in a tiring voice and realizes the call is from his father.

"Where are you son? We need to talk, and it can't be over the phone." Kraus instructed.

Jaden tells his dad he's in Columbus currently, but can meet him later. Jaden's dad instructs him to meet at Superior Deli for lunch around 12:30 p.m. Jaden looked at his watch, reading the current time of 3:30am. He assures his dad he would meet him for lunch. Jaden then ends his call and turn towards Carmella. Her back faces his chest, but she wasn't asleep.

"Will you be me leaving soon?" Carmella asks.

Jaden sighs and responds, "We still have time for another fuck session. That's if you're game for it?"

Carmella lets out a soft moan as she turned towards Jaden. "She's always wet for you." Carmella began kissing Jaden as they made love.

Later that morning Jordan was meeting with Agent Ford. She invited Jordan into her office for a sit down and to inform him of his additional duties as an ODI agent.

"I forgot to tell you that you're being assigned to a federal task force as your miscellaneous duties of an ODI agent. The agency of your assignment will be with Secret Service. Not to worry, you won't be guarding the President. However, you'll be assigned to their covert Organized Crime Task Force. Your background has already been sent over and cleared for a TS/SCI status. Drive over to the Cleveland Field office and meet with Assistant Special Agent in Charge Tom Warfield. He will be the ASAC overseeing the task force. I told you when you joined; we're a unique unit of the Governor's Office. Our authority is unapproachable and so is our integrity. Don't fuck this up. Now go be a G-Man." Ford instructed.

Jordan left Agent Ford's office with his orders and b-lines directly to Tyler's desk for a quick chat. Curious of his miscellaneous duties, he wanted to converse with Tyler. Tyler was Jordan's go to, he trusted him more than anyone else of ODI.

"Are you assigned to a task force?" Jordan asks.

Tyler smiles and acknowledges Jordan's question with an upward head nod. He then replies, "Everyone under Ford's leadership is assigned to one, even her. She's assigned to the FBI-Joint Terrorism Task force. I'm assigned to DOD-Intelligence Task Force. Agent Duncan is assigned to the DEA-Caribbean Task Force and your boy Stanzell is with USMS-Special Organized Group Task Force. Now you're being assigned to Secret Service- Special Enforcement Unit Task Force."

Jordan was curious of how Tyler New his assignment before he did. "Did Ford already tell you about my assignment?" Jordan asks.

Tyler smiles again and replied, "You're taking former agent and brother, Mookiah Graham's spot. He was assigned to Secret Service. This is why we train the way we do."

Jordan felt honored to be in his current position and embraced this opportunity to serve his country. Jordan smiled at Tyler as he left the duty room in route to the Secret Service field office.

Thirty minutes later, Jordan arrives at the Secret Service field office. "Good morning ma'am. I'm James Jordan, here to meet with ASAC Warfield."

The secretary asked Jordan to sign-in as she replied, "He will be with you momentarily, sir."

Jordan nodded and smile at the secretary's response. He then chose a seat and waited for ASAC Warfield. As Jordan sat patiently, he observed the presidential photos of our previous presidents in office. One particular photo caught his attention. It was the photo of Ronald Reagan and his Secret Service detail. The photo stood out among others affixed to the wall. Jordan rose from his seat and approached the photo for closer observation. The agent who stood left of Reagan was posed in the photo as if he was an action figure. Jordan chuckled upon viewing the photo. He then felt a presence behind him.

"That was my favorite photo." ASAC Warfield stated.

Jordan turned around to identify the mysterious voice and learned it was the agent in the photo. He stood surprise in a moment of silence. ASAC Warfield extends his hand to break Jordan's silence and the weird feeling he was experiencing.

"I am Assistant Special Agent-in-Charge, Warfield."

Jordan shook his hand and commented, "I never met anyone from the presidential detail.

ASAC Warfield smiled and replies, "you'll get used to it. It won't be your last. Now, let's get you up to speed with your new detail."

ASAC Warfield escorted Jordan to his office to discuss his duties. He went over the Standard Operational Procedures (SOP) with him. Warfield wanted Jordan to be clear in understanding his duties as a Task Force Agent. Warfield continued to advise Jordan of other requirements to maintain his existence on the task force.

"You will need to qualify under our training to maintain your Federal Clearance. All Secret Service Agents conduct weapon's training every thirty days to be above proficient. Although ODI have rigorous training, your proficiency here is how you maintain your position as a Secret Service Task Force Agent. Are we clear?" Warfield advised.

Concluding their meeting, ASAC Warfield had another Task Force Agent escort Jordan to their indoor range for immediate qualifications.

Later the afternoon around 12:30pm, Jaden sat down for lunch with Kraus at Superior Deli. He could see the concern look upon his father's face as Kraus took sips from a glass of orange juice.

"What's wrong dad?" Jaden asked.

Kraus replied, "Indictments son, indictments. Prosecutor McGarlin is aware of my operation at the gentlemen's club. He was trying to squeeze me for a payoff. Since I didn't adhere to his agreement, he subpoena me before a Grand Jury. Now if I don't testify, I'm looking at serious jail time."

Jaden looked his dad in the eye and told him not to worry about anything. "Pop, I'm going to take care of this. Stay close to your phone the next 48 hours. Jaden got up from the table and exited the restaurant.

Currently at the States Commissioner's Office, Commissioner Gordon was having a conference call with his constituents. Suddenly, a vibrating noise echoed from his desk drawer. Gordon retrieved the device from its secret location and saw an encrypted text message. Gordon decoded the sent message and read its contents.

"We have a problem with the City Prosecutor. Issues which can cause catastrophic blow backs to our operation. Deal with it or I will".

The message had no acknowledgement of its sender, but Gordon had a good idea who sent it. He then returned back to his conference call, advising his business partners he had to attend unforeseen matters of interest.

Meanwhile at the County District Attorney's Office, McGarlin's Secretary enters to inform him of Father Terry's arrival. Terry stood patiently at the door waiting to be invited in.

"Father Terry, come in please, welcome to my office. How might I be at service to you?" McGarlin greeted.

Terry advises he is having some permit problems. It seems a nuisance order issued upon Seven Bells skating rink was preventing a charitable event. He requested assistance from McGarlin to have the order removed and allow his church to sponsor a community event.

"Could I bother you to lift a nuisance order against Seven Bells Skating Ring? it would allow my church to facilitate a fundraising benefit for our intercity kids of Cleveland." Terry Requested.

McGarlin knew this would be an opportunity for him to enlist voters from Terry's congregation. Secured votes from Terry's church would assist him with further existence as a county politician. McGarlin was in favor of lifting the order as Terry saw him as another political ally.

"I will have the Sheriff come by today and take care of that for you." McGarlin stated.

"I hope your tip line receive the proper information, regarding our dear friend Commissioner Gordon and his associate?" Father Terry uttered.

McGarlin chuckled to acknowledge it did. Father Terry tipped his head as an act of saying of "You're Welcome". He then turns around and exits McGarlin's office. McGarlin stood in silence displaying a cynical grin due to his alliance with Father Terry.

Speeding westbound on Highway I-90, Jordan had just completed his weapons qualification for the Secret Service Task Force. He's currently headed to CPD Headquarters to meet up with Korda from IT. Ten minutes later, Jordan is turning into the employee parking lot of headquarters. He exits his vehicle and takes the employee entrance into the building and head towards the IT division.

"Hey bro thanks for meeting me. I have this device that needs to be decrypted." Jordan stated as he shows Korda the device.

Korda thoroughly examines the device, checking for malware and hidden trojan horses. Upon finding no spy programming, he inserts the device in his encryption decoder. Jordan smiles while watching Korda be a nerd. The two have been friends since college and now colleagues in law enforcement.

"This may take a while. You might want to hang tight until it's done." Korda said.

Jordan decline the offer and advised he would be in the Chiefs office. Korda told Jordan he would text him when it's done. Jordan left the IT division and headed to meet with Jenkins.

Minutes later, Jordan is tapping upon the Chief's door to announce his presence. Jenkins invites him in for a sit down. Jenkins and Jordan were more than colleagues of law. They considered themselves as true friend of each other.

"Haven't seen you for a while, how's being a liaison treating you," asked Jenkins.

Jordan informed Jenkins he's doing well and that his credentials have increased to Federal status. Jordan showed Jenkins his task force ID from Secret Service. "I'm currently assigned to the Secret Service Task Force, in addition to my assignment with ODI."

Jenkins chuckles and replied, "So you're wearing three badges now. I wouldn't be mad at you if you left CPD entirely and pursued your career with ODI. Sometimes you need to step back to get a clearer picture ahead."

Jenkins could see Jordan was weighing his options. He knew Jordan was the kind of guy who always thought ahead. Jordan knew Jenkins could sense he may be leaving the department. As an inducement to conversation, Jenkins reaches into his desk drawer. He then pulls out a fifth of Jameson and pours its contents into two glasses.

"You sure know how to bring enlightenment to a conversation," stated Jordan.

"Yes, I do have my ways. I've also noticed your success within this department. I realize your experience is far more then CPD. Should ODI offer you a permanent spot off your contingent position, don't hesitate to take it. Opportunities like yours come few and far between. Besides, you don't owe this department shit. You've gave them everything, by giving your soul and losing a daughter behind it. Salvage what you have and move on. No one could be mad at you, not even me," exclaimed Jenkins.

Jordan shared drinks and conversation for minutes onto minutes. Suddenly, He received a text reading, "encryption done."

Jordan finished his glass of Jameson and departed the Chief's company. He returns back to the IT Division to confer with Korda. As Jordan walks into Korda's lab, he could see the excitement on his friend's face. The look which resembles "I did it."

"Ok, what do you have for me brother?" Jordan asks.

Korda advises he manage to identify a location for a future drug transaction.   Jordan displayed a pensive impression upon his face as he thought of a strategy to intercept the drugs. Korda continued debriefing more intelligence about the device.

 "These guys are smart, not to put all of their eggs in one basket. Whomever you recovered this device from is scheduled to meet with a contact identified as Naza. The meet is in three days at approximately 20:00 hours. I suggest you get moving on this, if you're planning to set up a surveillance detail." Korda instructed.

An hour later, Jordan met his team at Agent Duncan's law office. The team had a covert office there for inclusive meetings. Jordan introduced what he'd learn on the encrypted device. He indicated to setting up video surveillance for intelligence gathering. Agent Tyler suggested getting there early to secure a covert position to monitor their targets.

Three days later at approximately 20:00 hours, Jordan and his team set up surveillance in the middle of Lake Erie, three clicks south of international waters. They observed a go boat breaching Canadian waters and headed to Pelee Island. Agent Tyler launched an aerial drone to monitor activity from the sky. The covert device captured the boat's travel and identified two subjects onboard.

The occupants landed their boat upon the night shores of Pelee. They then exited the boat carrying large bags with undisclosed contents. As the subjects walked further onto shore, they were met by three additional subjects from the island. Ensuing a brief conversation between parties, drone surveillance secured video coverage of an exchange taking place. The primary subjects then reentered their boat and headed back towards U.S waters.

Jordan and Tyler maintained surveillance from a distance, keeping their covert position intact. Thirty minutes later, the primary subjects reached the Port of Sandusky Harbor, in the City of Sandusky, Ohio. Agent Ford accompanied by Agents Duncan and Stanzell took over surveillance once the targets reached dry land.

"Be advised, we have the targets entering a black SUV, Ohio plate #ATC-441. It's confirmed the cargo from the boat has been uploaded into the vehicle" Agent Tyler radioed.

"I will radio for your additional support once we reach the city limits of Cleveland." Ford responded.

She then instructed Tyler and Jordan to drive the agency boat to the Cleveland Harbor and dock it. Ford and Duncan were teamed up in one vehicle as the first leg of the surveillance. Agent Stanzell was in another vehicle as the second leg of surveillance. Ford instructed Stanzell to keep over watch for any recon vehicles and be prepared to trade off in the surveillance detail.

An hour later, Tyler and Jordan arrived at the Cleveland Harbor. They quickly secured the agency boat and transferred all their duty equipment into an undercover vehicle. Tyler then sat behind the steering wheel of their vehicle. He began reminiscing moments of Mookie's death. The voice of his late partner echoed in his head.

[Mookie's Voice]: "I have a black Dodge Charger on my right. Oh shit, shots fired, shots fired."

Tyler could picture the vivid exchange of gunfire, which ended "Mookie's" life. He then snapped back to current time and looks over at Jordan. Tyler felt choked as he tries to formulate words. In a couple attempts to speak, Tyler has to clear his throat. Finally, his voice comes to him and he's able to speak.

"Bro, not trying to tell you how to do your job and all. But I don't want to lose another partner. Stay alert for vehicles trailing our six!" Tyler explained.

Jordan nodded his head and tapped the top of their vehicle to signal let's go.

It's 9pm in the Fourth District of Cleveland. Detective Carter of Cleveland's HTS-Division is investigating a drug related homicide outside the Juva De nightclub. Witnesses reported the victim was gunned down after being confronted by a drug dealer. Conflicting details indicated the shooting took place inside of the premises. Carter observes a small blood trail showing directional travel from inside the club. Carter's intuition encouraged him to interview employees of the establishment and learn why the deceased was found dead outside. As Carter walked inside, he found more small drippings of blood confirming the incident took place inside and not out. He further noticed the blood trail ending six feet from the bar area. Carter approached the bar, displaying his badge and requesting to speak with Johnnie B.

Johnnie B is a Haitian from Miami with ties to the criminal enterprise, "Zoe Pound". The Juva De, which he own and operated was in a neighborhood associated to Harvard Heights Kings. HHK agreed to let Johnnie B operate in the Harvard area as long as he paid rent. While Detective Carter awaits the arrival of Johnnie B, a female bartender slips him a napkin with writing on it.

"The dead guy you're investigating was shot by Carla. She's in the kitchen, preparing the bar menu." The napkin read.

Immediately Carter radioed to officers outside, requesting them to secure a perimeter around the establishment and to come inside to search for a suspect.
Four CPD Officers came inside to assist Carter, while additional officers entered to secure patrons for later questioning by police.

"Everyone is to stay until questioned by an officer. Make sure you get a full disclosure from each witness," said Carter.

Carla who was suspected of shooting the victim was still in the kitchen when she heard Carter give his instructions to the officers. Fearing the officers were closing in on her, she climbed her 5-foot 120-pound frame into the kitchen air ducts. Her plan was to maneuver outside of the police perimeter for an escape. Carter and his men headed for the kitchen area looking for their only suspect. He was hoping to learn why she shot the unknown victim.

As Carter and two uniform officers inter the kitchen, Carla closes the vent behind her. She then sucks in her stomach and gently crawls through the air duct.

"Where is this bitch," said Carter in a scoffing voice.

He instructed officers to continue their search of the club. Carla took a slow and deep breath to relieve the tension from her body. She suppressed the overwhelming stress within herself to counter her involuntary muscle reaction. Carla continued crawling through the ducts quietly as to draw no attention to her location. Upon moving several feet through the air ducts, Carla came to her destination of escape. She placed her feet against the vent and gave a powerful thrust to disengage it from the wall. The vent fell several feet before making a clinging sound as it hit the floor.

Carla began wriggling her arms and shoulders free of the air duct. She then looked down to notice a substantial drop to the floor. Her further observation found a mail hamper fifteen feet below to her right. Carla focused on the drop, aiming her body to align perfect within the hamper. As she hung-dropped from the air duct, Carla rotated her legs around and landed inside the hamper. Crawling out of the hamper, Carla escaped through a door into an alley. She observed her getaway car waiting for her. An unknown driver was parked in a black Cadillac CTS facing the Main Street of Harvard. Carla opened the vehicle's passenger door and enters. A CPD Officer identified her as the bartender wanted for questioning. He ordered Carla to stop moving, but she ignored his commands.

The vehicle's driver-side window declined partially, concealing its driver. The driver then extended a weapon from his window, firing several rounds in the direction of police. Officers scattered for nearby cover as the sounds of screeching tires against pavement echoed in the night.

Detective Carter exists the club to observe a cloud of smoke from the subject's vehicle upon its escape.

Carter transmits across his police radio for assistance, "Control this is John Sam-9, requesting assistance in the area of Harvard and 178th street. I have a murder suspect fleeing the scene of the "Juva De" night club. Vehicle is described as a Black Cadillac, Ohio plate #HHK4LF, occupying one female subject, driver unknown."

Sirens began wailing as multiple police cars searched for the black Cadillac in question. In desperation to capture Carla and her driver, Carter reaches out to Jordan for additional support.

On this same evening, DA McGarlin sits alone at the Cleveland Chop House enjoying a steak dinner and red wine. He glances at his Merlot through a clear glass, swirling its contents and examining how many wine legs appear. McGarlin smiles upon observing four legs, indicating the potency of alcohol per glass is to his liking. He then slices into a 28-ounce Prime Rib steak, tasting a rare flavor of carnivorous pleasure. McGarlin washes down the marinated juices with another sip of red wine. As he places his glass upon the table, he looks up to an uninvited guest.

 "May I help you friend?" McGarlin asks.

The mysterious man wore a business sweater and Fedora hat slanted forward to conceal his identity. The mystery man chuckled when questioned by McGarlin as he replied in his Haitian accent.

"Usually I seal tee fate of me targets by making tem an accident for tee news. In your case, I must make a statement."

McGarlin's face expressed serious concern to the mystery man's comment and before he could react, he collapsed backwards into his chair. The force penetration of a bullet to McGarlin's forehead concluded his dinner for the night. The mystery man immediately departed the restaurant. Onlookers observed blood pouring from the lifeless body of McGarlin as they gathered around his table.

Jordan's cellphone began vibrating with Carter's cell number in his LCD screen. He scoffed, followed by a pause before answering Carter's call.

"Looks who's calling daddy." Jordan answered.

"Trust me, if I didn't need you, I wouldn't have called. However, we both could benefit from this call." Carter replied.

CHAPTER SEVEN: TRAINING DAY (PART 2)

Carter is standing in front of the Juva De talking to Jordan on his cell. He has to end his conversation due to an incoming call from dispatch. CPD Dispatch advises him of another homicide in the Cleveland area.

"Sir are you available to take another call. We have a 419 at the Cleveland Chop House. The Chief is requesting you to handle this one and pass your current investigation over to Robbery-Homicide." Dispatch advised.

Carter sighed but took his orders like a good little Detective. He then gave Jordan a quick text and ask for his help again.

"Bro, I need your help. Bodies are dropping like flies tonight. Hit me back!"

10:45 pm on the West Bank of the Cleveland Flats, Agent Ford and her team trails the black SUV to an abandoned warehouse. The listed premises sat a block away from the Mirage nightclub. Agent Stanzell set up adjacent of Ford and Duncan's vehicle. Jordan and Agent Tyler were shortly to arrive. Stanzell began taking photos from a distance. He identified the occupants as Johnnie B and Jaden Kraus. The subjects were unloading duffel bags from their vehicle to carry inside the warehouse.

"Did you guys see that?" Ford stated as she transmitted across her two-way radio.

"We need to get a closer look inside." Stanzell said.

"L-42 to L-257, how far are you guys out," transmits Ford upon her radio.

"257 to 42, we'll be approaching in five," responded Tyler.

Ford instructed a triangular approach to the premises but did not advise any personnel to breach until Agents Tyler and Jordan arrive.

Just as Tyler was transmitting across the radio, Jordan was responding to a text from Detective Carter.

"I'll hit you back in a minute. In the middle of an operation."   Jordan texted back.

Tyler and Jordan's vehicle arrived at the north side of the warehouse, covering its back entrance.

"42 be advised, we're on-scene. What's your location?" Tyler asked.

Ford advised they were at the front entrance of the premises. She indicated of breaching from their position with Tyler and Jordan covering the north end. Tyler advises to hold position and let his drone breach from an open window of the warehouse.

"Let's get an inside view of our subject's location." Tyler stated.

Tyler sets the drone in motion, navigating it through an open window to locate its targets. Drone surveillance captured the primary subject's meeting with two additional targets. Johnnie B opened their duffle bags and displayed several packages, which appeared to be narcotics.

"Have your drone located our targets?" Ford Transmits across her radio.

Tyler advises the targets had been located. He indicated the drone captured video of suspected narcotics packaged for sale.

"Continue monitoring their activity for PC. Duncan and Stanzell, fall back into perimeter surveillance." Ford instructed.

The listed agents reentered their vehicles, preparing for mobile surveillance at the subject's next movement. Agent Tyler's drone continued monitoring the subject's activity.

"So, do you like this product or what?" Johnnie B asked.

"We'll see after your shit is tested for purity. You can examine the money for a true count." Unidentified Male-1 replied.

"Ah, Blue, which means your shit is right. I like that." Unidentified Male-2 stated.

"Yeah, the monies right too." Jaden commented.

"I guess we have a deal my nigga?" Johnnie B says.

"You blacks use that word so loosely but become offended when someone like me uses it." Unidentified Male-2 said.

Johnnie B sucks his teeth and replies, "You two fucks may be Irish, but you're no fucking Kennedy. You can believe that shit! Bro let's step before I pop a cap in this bitch ass nigga."

Johnnie B and Jaden gathered the duffel bags containing money as they departed the warehouse. Subjects one and two stayed behind to secure their product, allowing distance between their new business associates.

"I don't trust those niggers!" Unidentified Male -2 said.

"Fuck who they are, I trust the product they supply. Don't let your back-wood prejudice fuck up our connection, nigga!" Unidentified Male-1 stated as he chuckled.

Jaden and Johnnie B were securing the exchanged duffle bags in their vehicle as they were being observed by Ford's team. Ford then transmits across the radio, informing her team to start the mobile surveillance. She instructed Tyler and Jordan to follow the remaining subjects in the warehouse. The vehicle occupying Jaden and Johnnie B drives off from the warehouse parking lot, followed in a distance by Ford, Duncan and Stanzell. Tyler retreats his drone and prepare for the remaining subjects to exit. Minutes later, two male-whites exits with duffle bags and enters a white Chevy Impala. The Chevy Impala travels one block east to the Mirage nightclub and enters its parking lot.   The male-whites exit their vehicle with bags in hand and enters the club. Agents Tyler and Jordan parallel park across from to the club. Their unobstructed view allowed them to capture long range photos of the duffle bags being transported inside the Club.

"These digital pics will give us PC to get a warrant." Jordan stated.

Tyler informs Ford of what they captured on video. She instructed them to maintain surveillance from their current location and not to breach the club.

Tyler began fumbling around with the video from his drone, cropping facial photos to run through a recognition database. After cropping the photos, Tyler then takes a small latent kit from his glove compartment.

"What are you doing?" Jordan asked.

"Some old fashion police work." Tyler replied.

Tyler exited their vehicle, leaving Jordan behind to continue his photo surveillance. Tyler crepes discreetly across the street and into the small parking lot of Mirage night club. He further approaches the subject's vehicle and began applying small amounts of Black latent powder upon it. Tyler continues his efforts of evidence collection by swabbing each door and handles of the subject's vehicle. He further applies latent tape to secure possible prints of the subjects. Jordan takes a couple of photos of Tyler lifting prints as documented evidence. Tyler returns to their vehicle and continues surveilling for illicit activity.

Currently at the Cleveland Chop House, Carter examines the death scene of DA McGarlin. He turns to an employee of the establishment and request the presence of their manager. Stella Calzoni answers the call of Detective Carter.

"Evening Detective, how may I be of assistance?" Stella inquired.

"How about your name? Carter asked.

"It's Stella, Stella Calzoni. What might be your name Detective?"

Carter smiled as his eyes examined the sexy and curving body of lady Calzoni. He further licked his lips like a lion would do before pouncing its prey. Lady Calzoni smiles as she observes Carter's premature lust for her.

"It's Kyle Carter and I noticed no visible cameras in your establishment. Is that for preferred privacy?" Carter asked.

"Kyle, may I call you Kyle?" Lady Calzoni asked.

"I prefer last names in reference of one another." Carter instructed.

Lady Calzoni smiled at Carter and complied with his request. She then explains her establishment caters to exquisite clientele who requests unapproachable privacy due to their client's line of work. In conversation with Lady Calzoni, he notices her last name to be common which the notorious Cleveland Mob Boss, Michael Calzoni.

"You wouldn't be related to the prestigious Michael Calzoni?" Carter asks.

"Indeed I am. But my brother's world is his alone. I share nothing of what he does. So please, I wish you not speculate my character with his events, Detective!" Lady Calzoni replies.

 A smirk appears upon Carter's face. He looks away, examining the restaurant's structure and requests to look around its premises.   Lady Calzoni agrees to Carter's request.

"Just let me know if there any locked areas you wish to enter." Lady Calzoni sexually suggested.

Calzoni knew her sex appeal had Carter's interests, an advantage which she could exploit at any time. Carter's eyes examine Lady Calzoni's body before departing her presence. She then walks away and leaves Carter to his investigation.

Currently on the other side of Cleveland, Ford's surveillance team tracks Jaden and Johnnie B to Cranwood Apartments. The agents observed their targets parking before Building-G of the complex. Jaden and Johnnie B takes the duffle bags from their suburban and enters the building. Stanzell gets out on foot to observe what apartment they're going enter. He's able to witness them entering apartment 204 of Building-G. An emergency exit sign hangs directly in front of the apartment. Stanzell affixes a small camera onto it, hoping to capture any activity from the dwelling. He then returns to his vehicle, alerting Ford and Duncan about the surveillance camera.

"Hey guys, are you getting a live feed from my camera?" Stanzell asks.

"Your feed is active and clear." Ford replied.

Back at the restaurant, Carter is about to leave his crime scene when he gets a text message from Detective Eugene Glover of Homicide.

"Your dead body at Juva De was identified as a Melvin Miller, Special Investigator for DA McGarlin."

Carter scratches his head in curiosity of why someone would kill Miller. He was even more curious of who killed the DA. He then opens a new message to text. The text message was authored to Jordan.

"Bro, can you look into two homicides that may be related. DA McGarlin and his Special Investigator were killed tonight. Call me when you have something."

Jordan and Tyler are still surveilling activity outside the Mirage night club. Jordan looks at his cellphone as he feels it vibrating. He then muted the message to read at a later time. Tyler taps Jordan on his shoulder, alerting him of the subject's exiting the Mirage and heading to their vehicle.

"Heads up bro, our mopes are leaving the club."

The subjects got into their Vehicle and exited the parking lot. Agents Tyler and Jordan followed them in a near distance. As Tyler tailed the subject's vehicle, Jordan read the text from Carter. He then called Carter to learn what was so urgent.

"Bro, it's about time you got back to me. I have two separate homicides I believe may be related." Carter stated.

Jordan asked Carter why he believed his homicides were related. Carter informed him that the deceased victims were employees of the county. Carter highlighted the DA and his special investigator were the deceased. Jordan became concerned of Carter's news. He invited him to come by the field office on the next day.

"My team and I will review whatever intelligence you have bro." Jordan stated.

He then hears Agent Ford's call sign transmit across their radio. Jordan terminates his call with Cater to answer Ford's transmission.

 "L-257 to 42, go ahead." Jordan answers.

She informs Jordan of her location regarding the money drop. Ford indicated remote surveillance was in placed to capture and identify subjects related to the drug money. She instructed Jordan to continue their surveillance detail and meet tomorrow for a complete debriefing. Jordan acknowledged her instructions and continued their current assignment.

The next morning, Detective Carter along with Agents Tyler and Jordan met at the county morgue. The medical examiner was going over his findings for cause of death regarding DA McGarlin and Special Investigator Miller.

"Your two victims have similar causes of death, GSW determined their demise. The Investigator died within minutes from a GSW to the heart. DA McGarlin died instantly from a GSW to his frontal lobe. I sent the extracted rounds to ballistics. I'll know more when the results return," stated the medical examiner.

Carter and the Agents took detail notes from the autopsy and deliberated on possible leads to their investigation. They then left the coroner's office and headed to the ODI field office.

It's 10:00 am and Kraus is getting ready for the lunch crowd at his Gentlemen's Club. Kraus is sitting in his office going over financial transactions when he hears a knock on his door.

"Who the fuck is it?" Kraus shouted.

The door opens and enters Father Terry. He greets Kraus with a pleasant tone, but Kraus dismisses his kind gesture and inquires about his visit to the club.

"Why are you here? The money drop isn't due until Friday. You're two days early and your presence in my establishment gives a sacrilegious appearance, don't you think?" Kraus' exclaims.

"My appearance has nothing to do with our business in hand. It should concern you when government officials are showing up dead, because that brings problem to the both of us. I don't like frivolous problems Kraus!" Father Terry stated.

Kraus sucked his teeth and states, "Government official huh? I would assume you're speaking about that dead DA and his flunky Investigator. Rumor has it you paid the DA a visit and now he's dead. That's suspect to me!"

A mist of tension begins to fill the air. Terry displays a grimace look as he clears his throat. He then selects his next few words carefully, knowing the idea of trust between the two is becoming a mystery.

"The DA and I were speaking of a charity event for the inner-city youth. His agreement to lift a nuisance order on the Seven Bells Skating rink was my only ploy. The death of DA McGarlin as so his Investigator, had nothing to do with my visit. You should clarify your information before dissemination. As for the money, have my shit ready. I want no delays in the transitioning of funds, you understand my friend." Terry stated.

Kraus draws in a sniff and nods his head to Terry's comment. Terry then leaves his office, using the back entrance to be unnoticed.

It's Noontime at the ODI field office, Agent Ford orders lunch for an in-house briefing. Detective Carter was in attendance with intentions of receiving help on his current cases.

"Agents, I called this 'Sit-Rep' to debrief on what we discovered and possibly lend some support to Detective Carter." Ford advised.

Carter opens the debriefing with his intelligence on the murders of Lopez, Fats Gillespie, Investigator Miller and DA McGarlin. He indicates all may be connected in some way. Carter suggested Lopez was killed because of her father's mob-ties. He reveals her as the daughter of Constantine Gordon, also known as the Ohio Liquor Commissioner and owner of Gordon's Cannery. Agent Ford interjects with her intelligence of Gordon being on the government's watch list for racketeering and illicit activities. She further indicated the U.S. Attorney's Office was considering Gillespie as a Secret witness against Commissioner Gordon due to his illicit activities.

"Gillespie was killed in his own home awaiting entry into the witness security. I believe Gordon had something to do with his death." Ford presumed.

Detective Carter continued with his facts, advising Gillespie was identified as a known associate of The Calzoni Family, local crime syndicate of the Cleveland Mafia. Carter then suggested Michael Calzoni, newly appointed mob boss, had Gillespie silenced for obvious reasons.

Agent Tyler began sharing intelligence photos taken from the abandoned warehouse in which they surveilled. He identified all four subjects in his photo array, "Mark Kraus, Timothy O'Hennesy, Jaden Kraus and Johnnie B.

"This makes since now. CPD Narcotics heard rumors of drugs being transported by liquor trucks throughout the city. Mark Kraus owns Kraus Gentlemen's Club. That club is suspect of prostitution and illegal gambling.   However, he's politically protected." Cater Exclaimed.

Jordan suggests an undercover operation to learn more and discover the source. He suggests to Ford of letting him go under as a Trinidadian national visiting friend's in Cleveland.

"How are you going to pull off that charade, being you're formally CPD?"   Agent Tyler stated.

Jordan informs his wife is a beautician with the art of forming different hair styles. He continued to say she could make him a Rastafarian wig, which could give him the optics for his Trinidadian cover.

"My identity can be altered through optics of using a wig. Plus, I have a nephew who's "Zoe Pound" and he can back my cover." Jordan explained.

Agent Ford liked the idea but knew Agent-In-Charge Walter Byers had to sign off on the op. Jordan saw this operation as his chance to become a permanent ODI Agent. Later that afternoon Agent Ford spoke candidly with AIC Byers. She informed him of the potential assignment with CPD.

  "You think our boy can pull this off. If he does, he would have completed his training day." AIC Byers stated.

Agent Ford supported the idea of Jordan going undercover. She assured Byers; Jordan had the skill set to complete his assignment. Byers gave Ford the ok to run her op. She then his office and immediately called the cellphone of Jordan.

  "Hey, our op is a go. Get with the rest of our team to go over an action plan." Agent Ford instructed.

CHAPTER EIGHT: FROM CATERPILLAR TO BUTTERFLY

"When this operation is over, you would have Transition from a Caterpillar to a Butterfly. Make no mistake, this cocoon process will be more dangerous than any CPD assignment you've ever worked. Make sure your 'A' game is better than any game you ever played." Agent Ford lectured.

Jordan displayed a nostalgic stare when responding to Agent Ford's short lecture. "I've been longing to be more then CPD. Protecting those in my community is bittersweet then becoming the product of my environment. Growing up in Cleveland I had two options, gang bang and sell dope or show the naysayers their segregation can't keep an honest Blackman down. I'm more than ready for this op. For my skill set is what you need to get this shit done. Let's do this!"

Ford smiles in assurance of Jordan's confidence. The two then exited her office into the "Duty room" for a team briefing. Indistinct chatter is occurring upon their entry. Ford commands the attention of the fellow agents and Detective Carter, who is also in attendance for this special meeting.

"Team, two days from now we will conduct a joint investigation with CPD on the premises of Juva De. Our goal is to learn how the murders of Gillespie, Lopez, Miller and DA McGarlin are related. We will further identify the network of this current drug distribution in our city. Rumor has it that local nightclubs may be involved with the dissemination of product." Ford advised.

Jordan stands up to speak before the agents about his part in the assignment.
"As you know, I will be the undercover agent in this op. My cover will be a Trinidadian national visiting the City of Cleveland. I will try to identify any primaries who can lead us to our murderer and potential drug distributors."

Detective Carter had a plan to implement Jordan's cover, by using a third-party contact known associated to the Juva De night club.
"I know a former CPD copper who's currently working patrol for GPD. He hangs out at the Juva De and knows a few employees of the establishment. He also has a thing for "Black Coffee". I figure we send a female undercover his way and lock him in as a CI." Carter informed.

Agent Duncan interjects and questioned Carter's plan of action. She had reservations of bringing new personnel onto the team at short notice. To bring ease to Duncan's concerns, Carter chooses her as the other operative for his plan.

"Agent Duncan will be driving west on Thornhurst towards East Boulevard. There will be a stop sign at that intersection. Duncan will roll through the stop sign, alerting the attention of our future CI. She will then continue north on East Boulevard towards Beechwood Road. The listed location is the Cleveland-Garfield Heights boarder, where we can have an unmarked observing the traffic stop." Carter explains.

"What makes you think this cop will go for my vehicle?" Duncan asks.

"Browning is a stat-hog who's looking to promote. I know this guy like the back of my hand. He's going to bite on the traffic violation. The key to this ruse is getting him to bite on the offer of taking your number. You think you can handle that?" Carter asks.

"Honey, I can sell water to a fish." Duncan replied.

"Let's hope this fish takes our bait. Now, once Browning takes your number, key your radio three times as a signal to intercept. Agent Ford and I will take it from there. We'll offer Browning to be a CI or be arrested for accepting a bribe." Carter concluded.

Jordan stood in agreement with Carter's reverse sting. He indicated Browning could be used to introduce his cover at the Juva De. The agents and Carter agreed to set their plan in motion the next day.

Later that evening, Jordan and Pam was having dinner at home. The couple were conversing about Jordan's new roll of becoming an ODI agent, leaving the life of an CPD cop in his rearview.

"You sure this is what you want," questioned Pam.

"What do you mean," asked Jordan.

"This cloak and dagger job," replied Pam.

"I'm getting bored with CPD. I feel my peak has been met there. Besides, this new job could bring unlimited opportunities for me." Jordan stated.

Pam saw the adventurous look in her husband eyes as he spoke of his new job. She didn't want to stop him from achieving his dreams or deter any goals he has set. To Pam, her husband was her everything and she wanted to be his world. Pam places her hand upon Jordan's, gently caressing him with her thumb. As Jordan continued to speak, Pam became captured by every word her husband spoke. Jordan saw the love of his life was more than a good listener, she was his comfort in this sinful world. The couple's conversation went on for hours, until retiring for the evening.

It's 3:30 pm on a Wednesday afternoon. The sun is about to set in two hours and a light breeze gently moves the leaves upon the trees. Officer Browning is sitting in a marked black and white police vehicle observing traffic at the intersection of East Boulevard and Thornhurst Avenue. Browning's vehicle is facing a northbound direction, sitting 100 feet southeast of the intersection. The flow of vehicle traffic was light with an average of one vehicle every five minutes to approach the intersection. At approximately 3:35 pm, a green Chevy Nova traveling west on Thornhurst failed to stop at the intersection monitored by Browning. The vehicle continued its travels as it turned right onto East Boulevard, traveling north towards Beachwood Road. Browning activates his emergency lights and pursues the vehicle. He yielded the vehicle just north of Beechwood Road and East Boulevard, in the jurisdiction of Cleveland.

Agents Tyler and Jordan were sitting in an unmarked police vehicle, monitoring Browning's traffic stop. They observed Officer Browning to approach the traffic violator's vehicle. Unknown to Browning it was Agent Duncan posing as a traffic violator. He began questioning her about the infraction and requested to view her driving information.

Instead of complying, Duncan offered her cell number in exchange of getting out of the ticket. Browning observed Agent Duncan to wear a fitting t-shirt, which displayed the imprint of her nipples due to no braw. The overwhelming sexual display by Duncan enticed Browning to take her offer.

Seconds after Browning accepts Duncan's offer, a CPD black and white arrived at his location. Detective Carter and Agent Ford exits the vehicle. Browning displays a confuse look as to why two plane clothes officers are exiting a marked police unit.

"How can I help you?" Browning asked.

Agent Ford chuckles at Browning's question as Carter stood by her side. She then identifies herself, displaying an ODI badge and presenting her title.

"What's an ODI Agent doing in a marked CPD vehicle?" Browning asked.

Agent Ford smiles again as Detective Carter identified himself and makes a direct quote.

"You just fucked yourself into a CPD-ODI Investigation."

Browning steps back from Duncan's vehicle and began to flex his authority, displaying he's the Alpha on scene.

"I know nothing about your investigation, but I do know you're interfering with my traffic stop." Browning stated.

Detective Carter plays a recording with Browning's voice accepting Duncan's cellphone number. Browning looks over at Duncan and she displays her credentials to him. He then looks at the phone number in his hand as he says, "Shit, what the fuck have I done!"

Agent Ford observes the "I'm fucked" look on Browning's face. She then offers him an "Olive Branch" out of his situation.

"You help us, and this situation goes away. Your department will never know about this unfortunate incident. Plus, you could get a commendation for your assistance in this operation." Ford offered.

Browning felt like a bug caught underneath a glass with limited air supply and everyone watching him die slowly. As a result of no other options, Browning agreed to cooperate. Agent Ford gave Browning her card and advised she would contact him later with further instructions.

"Should you fail to cooperate, I will have charges brought against you for accepting a bribe," explained Ford.

Browning scoffed at Fords comment but knew there was no other options for his survival in this classic trap. He then reentered his vehicle and left the scene without further incident.

It's Friday night and a light drizzle falls upon the City of Cleveland. Jordan looks down at his watch and it reads 8 p.m. He's is sitting in his personal vehicle outside of the ODI field office. Jordan began reminiscing thoughts of Jim as they said their temporary goodbyes. Suddenly his thoughts of Jim transitions into Pam's voice.

[Pam voice]: "You sure this is what you want?"

Pam's voice echoes over and over in Jordan's head until a picture of Kim's face appears. Jordan's heart then drops to his stomach and a single tear rolls down the right side of his cheek. He places his hands together, palm to palm and tilts his forehead towards them.

More tears descended upon Jordan's face as he whisper's a prayer: "Almighty God in heaven, watch over me as I protect those of innocents and the ones I love. Guide me with integrity and respect as I keep them safe both day and night. Light my path and keep it lit, as you guide my daily events through danger and grit. Although my body may be strong, but at times my mind can be weak. I ask you to erase those illicit thoughts that can knock me off my feet. For I am human, although my peers may place me above them. But when I take off this badge at night, I'm no different than her or him. She's my sister and he's my brother in arms, they're my family and friends I pledge to protect from harm.

My team's blood is my blood, their words are my thoughts I see. When I take on this mission tonight, I stand not alone, but in the company of thee. He who shed their blood to protect my life, I shall in return, shed my blood to protect their world. So, Lord give me strength and courage through my duty's end, for I pledge to protect my community, my family and my team, Amen!"

As Jordan raises his head, he could see Detective Carter's vehicle entering the parking lot. He further watched Carter exit the unmark vehicle he arrived in and enter the field office. Jordan waited until Carter was inside before exiting his vehicle. He didn't want to start a conversation due to his current state of mind. As he exited his vehicle, Jordan stood by the driver-side door and drew in a deep breath from the night air. He then exhaled, looking up at the night sky and smiled as though Kim was smiling down on him. Jordan finally walks inside to brief with other members of his team.

Several minutes later, Agent Ford enters the briefing room with Officer Browning of Garfield PD. Jordan is sitting at a table alongside with Tyler and Duncan. Agent Stanzell is setting up the power point for the briefing. He brings up a live feed of the Juva De night club from drone surveillance unit. Agent Ford starts off the briefing by introducing the live feed of Juva De.

"Alright, listen up everyone. As you can see, we have a live feed of our primary premises. According to our surveillance team onsite, no major targets have entered or exited the establishment. Jordan, Officer Browning will be inside of the Juva De prior to your arrival. When you arrive on scene, pick a secluded table and began to draw attention to your location. How do it, I don't care, but get all eyes on you. Browning will then talk up your background as a Trinidadian national looking for some stateside action." Ford explained.

Agent Stanzell takes over commentary giving instructions for Jordan's cover story.
"Jordan, when you enter the club, fine the ugliest female there is and make her feel special. Make her think she's your Beyonce and you're her Jay-Z. A woman who thinks she's on top of the world will bring the attention you need. If she has any friends with her, make sure they're having a good time too. You need no cock blocking with your introduction."

Jordan took mental notes on his cover story. All the excitement gave him the "bubble guts". He discreetly removes himself from the meeting and visits the restroom. Agent Ford gave closing remarks as indistinctive chatter became the ambience of the room.

In a surveillance van across the street from their targeted premises, Agent Ford is running command. She looks at her wat as it read 10:30 pm. Patrons are seen entering the Juva De. The ambience of the club is a "Hip-Hop" version with a twist of "Reggaeton". The DJ's music has everyone dancing and bobbing their head to his groove. Jordan finds an empty table adjacent from the DJ booth with a clear sight of the bar area. He could see Officer Browning sitting next to the serving well of the bar. A waitress approaches Jordan requesting his drink order.

"What can I get you?" The waitress asks.

 "White Rum on the rocks," stated Jordan.

"Where are you from," asked the waitress.

"Tobago," replied Jordan.

The waitress frowned and asked, "Where's that?"

Jordan smile and replied in a Caribbean ancient, "it's me home City of Trinidad. I from there, you know."

The waitress smile and stated, "You seem different. Not like these average Jokers in here. These nigga's in here be thirsty for Hennessey and shit. Sorry ass fucks excuse my language and shit. But these lames in here can't even tip a bitch."

Jordan saw a way to introduce his cover. "I can use this waitress as my mouthpiece." Jordan thought.

The waitress had a nice body, but a face of a horse. Jordan gave her a fifty-dollar bill and promised good tipping service should she keep his drinks fresh. The waitress smiled at Jordan before walking away to place his drink order.

Officer Browning conversed with Jordan's waitress as she placed several drink orders. He began to background Jordan's cover as a hitman working for the Caribbean Syndicate.

"You are making friends with that killer over there?" Browning asked.

The waitress chuckled as she continued placing her drink orders. She made light of Browning being jealous in response to his comment. "Why you hating Vanilla Ice? He's harmless and seems to have deep pockets unlike your broke ass. You need to take some lesson."

Browning chuckled, brushing off the waitress' comment with a smile. He continued to background Jordan's cover, presenting him as some kind of Trinidadian killer for hire. Browning convinced the waitress Jordan was suspected of a few homicides in the Cleveland area. The waitress didn't seem scared but appeared to be enthused about Jordan's street creds. After receiving Jordan's drink, she walked back to his table.

"Excuse me Mr. Mysterious, but what be your name," asked the waitress?

Jordan looked at the waitress from her tits down and back to her face. He prepared his words carefully, as he felt he had her on a hook like a fish.

"Malik, Malik St. Charles to be exact. Now, what is your name?"

The waitress smiled. She was enticed by the Caribbean accent Jordan displayed. Caressing her breast as a sexual overtone, the waitress identified herself as "Trina!"

Jordan sucked his teeth and said, "I call you Trini, like my country of Trinidad. Tee women there are so beautiful like you. You have boyfriend no? No matter no way, I take you from him. You be my queen and I treat you better than this. I wouldn't want my woman to work. Just sex me all day, while she feeds me."

Jordan's conversation caught the waitress attention. She was open to any and every word he said. Jordan's swagger influenced the waitress to brag about him to the other waitresses at the bar. Jordan was soon getting the attention he needed to support his cover.

Suddenly, Jordan heard Detective Carter's voice come across his ear wig. He mentioned the murder suspect wanted for Miller's death, had entered the building.

"Heads up, Carla just entered the building. She's identified as the murder suspect in Miller's death investigation. Say the word and we can take her into custody."

"Negative, stand-down on that. Let me work this bitch for some intelligence. Be sides, Miller is dead. No need to rush our investigation." Jordan commanded.

"Jordan, play this how you see fit. The team has your back." Ford instructed.

Agent Ford agree with Jordan's plan of action. She wanted to see how well he could play his cover against a seasoned criminal. Jordan gears up to introduce himself to Carla. He observed her to enter and walk behind the bar area where Browning sat. Browning is sipping on his drink and noticed how sexy Carla appeals to him. He calls out for her attention as Carla calculates the revenue figures of current bar sales.

"Excuse me, may I have my drink refreshed?" Browning asked.

Carla ignored Browning's attempt to communicate as she continued reviewing financial activity from the cash register. Trina returns to the service well to place more drink orders. She looks over at Browning who sat diagonal from Carla's position.

 "She's a sexy bitch isn't she." Trina stated.

"What makes you think I'm interested," replies Browning.

"I can tell, just by the way you're looking at her. Kind of how I'm looking at Malik, answers Trina.

"You're on first name basis with a hired killer?" Browning asks.

Browning and Trina's conversation catches Carla's attention. Carla paused from her managerial duties to interrupts their conversation.

"Trina, I'm sure you have drink orders to fill instead of cup-caking with your boyfriend over there. What I tell you about mixing work and sex? Give me his order and I'll take it to him. You can fuck him on your own time." Carla stated.

Trina complied without hesitation of Carla's request. She wanted no conflict with her boss, due to Carla's reputation of being a ruthless bitch. Carla made a drink for Jordan and took it to him.

Jordan observed Carla's approach. He envisioned Carla as a sexual treat, while watching her curving hips sway from side to side as she carried his drink in hand. Carla then leans forward to place his beverage on the table. Jordan peered his head around Carla's body to observe her tight fitting, but round ass. Carla observes him staring from her peripheral as she sat his drink under a napkin.

"What happened to my waitress?" Jordan asked.

"I prefer my employees to not mix personal affairs with business operations. Besides, I see the way you're staring at my ass. So, I will be serving your drinks until you're done!" Carla replied.

"So professional, so firm, what did I do to get such direct treatment?" Jordan asked.

"It's Malik, right?" Carla inquired.

Carla stared down at Jordan as she waited for his answer. Jordan examined the exquisite features of Carla as he made her wait for his answer.

"We can stare at each other all night. What is it you're looking for in my club?" Carla demanded.

Jordan took Carla's question as an intro to why he's there. Again, he prepared his words very carefully with the thought of Carla being a true killer. Jordan wanted Carla to believe his cover without fault in his attempt.

"I'm new to the City and looking for a way to extend my business," said Jordan.

Carla scoffs at Jordan's intro and replies, "Fuck your game, you're not new to the City. That half ass cop over there made you for some hired hand. Is that true?"

Jordan slightly paused before answering Carla. He was going to play off the cover Browning laid out for him.

"My business would only be with Johnnie B. I don't know you." Jordan stated.

Carla readjusted her posture from direct to inquisitive. She became curious of how Jordan knew Johnnie B. As a businesswoman with hood mentality, Carla didn't want to mess up any future business operations.

"How do you know Johnnie B and what makes you think he would do business with you?" Carla asked.

"You're fucking wasting my time. It's my employer who's interested in Johnnie B. Tell him I was sent by Caribbean Jay and if he's interested, holla' back at this number."

Jordan slams a Ben Franklin upon the table with his contact digits. He then got up and walk over to Trina, giving her another fifty-dollar bill for her services. Jordan looks back at Carla and sucked his teeth before walking out of the door. Carla collected the Ben Franklin with Jordan's contact digits.

The Cleveland night brings drizzling rain as Jordan drives to meet up with his team. He turns into an empty parking lot at JFK High School and parks next to a blacked-out utility van. Jordan exits his vehicle to enter the van.

"So, what do you think? Can this Carla deliver what we need? Is she the key to unlock our murder mysteries?" Agent Ford asks.

"She's the box that holds the key. I sensed she's Johnnie B's main bitch. Johnnie B is our key to these murders and much more," stated Jordan.

Jordan advised when he mentioned the name 'Caribbean Jay' to Carla, her eyes and body posture indicated she was the connection he needed.

"I hope you're right my friend. I'm not ready to lose another team member. Johnnie B is a Haitian who doesn't have a problem killing anyone, no matter if they're law enforcement." Stanzell stated.

"Which is why the name Caribbean Jay was mentioned as my employer. He's my nephew from Zoe Pound. His name carries a lot of weight and respect for my cover, it's backed tight." Jordan replied.

"What's your game plan," asks Tyler?

Jordan explained he would introduce his cover as a major weed distributor supported by Caribbean Jay. He continued his argument of stating he's looking for a coke distributor with good product to lace his marijuana stock.

"For a new guy, you're pretty innovative with this undercover shit," said Agent Duncan.

Jordan smiles at the approval of his colleague, but he didn't let his pre-accomplishment distract him from having a backup plan. Since his existence at ODI, Jordan became closer to Agent Tyler than any other agent of his team. He considered Tyler to be genuine with his acceptance into the unit. He asks Tyler to meet him at the "Chicken Shack" to talk shop, concluding the briefing. Agent Ford instructed the team to meet tomorrow morning for a full disclosure with AIC Byers.

Currently at the "Chicken Shack", a host seats Jordan and Tyler before taking their orders. After being seated, Jordan ordered ten wings with sauce and an order of fries. He further ordered a shoulder sandwich for Tyler.

"Thanks bro, for the midnight snack. So, what did you want to talk about?" Tyler asked.

"I'm thinking a backup plan is needed just in case this meet goes south." Jordan advised.

Tyler agreed to Jordan's suggestion. He indicated of having Johnnie B meet him at the Chicken Shack. Tyler jokes about Jordan ordering Curry-rice and Goat, due to it being a favorite Caribbean dish. Jordan chuckled at Tyler's comment. He knew Tyler was joking around to lighten his stress about the op.

Seriously bro, what if he declines my suggestion on the meeting location?"   Jordan asked.

Tyler scoffed before replying, "Then take an executive approach and tell him you'll meet at the Juva De. No exceptions! If he says no, hang up the call and we go to plan C."

Jordan frowned and asked Tyler what was plan C. Tyler massaged his face for a moment while staring at the table. Jordan could see he was in a pensive state of mind and didn't want to disturb his thought process. Tyler then looks up at Jordan, sucks his teeth and makes a profound statement.

"Bag and grab the mother-fucker. Take his bitch ass to one of our safe houses and convince him to cooperate. You know, show him some of that thug-life!" Tyler stated.

"I like that shit. It just might work. Sometimes you have to change shit up." Jordan pondered.

Tyler chuckled, "Yeah, change some shit up. Let's bounce, I have some sex to lay up in."

Jordan and Tyler exited the restaurant, going their separate ways for the night.

It's 7:30 a.m. and the sound of a vibrating cellphone awakens Johnnie B from his slumber. He looks around to locate the device and observes his naked girlfriend lying next to him. Her backside bares to him as she continues to sleep. Johnnie B takes a moment to smile at her beauty and then returns looking for his phone. He finds it vibrating phone in a pair of cargo pants on the bedroom floor.

"Who 'tis?" Johnnie B answered.

Carla's impatient voice projects from Johnnie B's phone. Her nagging tone irritates his ears.

"it's me, you blood clot!" Carla responded.

Johnnie sucks his teeth and replies back, "Bitch, what do you want at 'tis hour. It better be good, you know! I have sex in bed waiting for me."

Carla sighs and replies, "You're an ignorant fuck! I'm calling your black ass, because some Trini mother fucker came into the club last night asking for you. He dropped the name Caribbean Jay, as if that meant something when asking for your ass. You know a mother fucker of that name?"

The name Caribbean Jay grabs Johnnie's attention. He takes his conversation into the living room away from his sleeping guest.

"What did tis Trini look like? Did he have any Zoe Pound tats," asked Johnnie?

Carla advised she observed no tattoos. Jordan wore a trench coat and a turtleneck to hide any noticeable marks. She indicated he wanted to meet Johnnie B and left his number to be contacted. Johnnie B saved Jordan's number in his contacts after ending his call with Carla. He then returns to the company of his female guest.

"Is that club for me," asked the female guest?

Johnnie B chuckled as he engaged his guest for morning love. Sounds of pleasurable sex echoed from their bodies colliding intensely. The soft moans of his female guest fades into the background of their early morning.

The time is 8:25 am at the Field Office of ODI, AIC Byers is meeting with Agent Ford's Team. Stanzell begins with his opening statements:

"Last night we combined the joint efforts of ODI and CPD.   Our investigation targets a large drug distribution which may be associated to the high-profile murders of DA McGarlin, Special Investigator Miller of the DA's office and Tina Lopez. We believed the death of Agent Graham may also be associated to this investigation as well."

The assumption of Agent Graham's death being associated to the murders of Lopez, Miller and McGarlin, indicated some type of closure to the brutal death of a fellow agent. Byers and his team of agents wanted nothing more than to capture the assailants responsible. Detective Carter gave insight as to why Graham's death may be related.

 "Agents Tyler and Graham stumbled across a secret trafficking operation, involving liquor and narcotics. The day you guys were sitting on that stolen truck, Robbery-Homicide were investigating its disappearance from Gordon's Cannery. The fact Commissioner Gordon owned the aforementioned establishment gave suspicion of his daughter's death and the stolen trailer being connected. CPD was a day behind tracking the truck and its trailer. It wasn't until Agent Graham's demise when the pieces became clear."

Agent Tyler eyes became watery during the briefing. The death of his former partner was still fresh to him. Agent Duncan walks over to give Tyler a hug for support. It pained her to see him hurting.

Carter continued with his dissemination of facts. He formed an opinion that narcotics were being transported in its liquid form, posing as alcohol and later dehydrated into powder for distribution. Carter's assumption wasn't wrong and the idea of Gordon Cannery having distribution authority in three adjoining states, made a lucrative business opportunity for drug dealers.

 "This is where I come in!" Jordan stated.

Jordan indicated Juva De has been under watch by CPD-Narcotics for drug distribution. He revealed to have made contact with a bartender identified as Carla. Jordan indicated Carla took his contact information to pass on to her associate, Johnnie B. Agent Stanzell identified Johnnie

B as the owner of the Juva De nightclub. He then indicates Johnnie to be an associate of the Harvard Heights Kings, also known as HHK.

"HHK would never let Johnnie B operate in their hood without a price. I believe protection of some sort, may be included for product to be sold." Stanzell stated.

"Well it seems you guys have some pertinent intelligence here. Let's piece it all up and make some arrests," stated Byers.

The team agreed and as always, Agent Ford gave her closing remarks before concluding the meeting.

It's 9:15 a.m. and Commissioner Gordon is on the bench facilitating court. He and his Deputy Commissioners are conducting a sanction hearing on "Jonas Chicken and Beer." It appears the owner's son sold beer to a minor during the sale of Fried chicken wings.

"Counselor how does your client plea?"   Commissioner Gordan Asks.

"My client plea's not guilty Commissioners. He further asks the courts for leniency due to his status of being a law student. A conviction would be critical to his chances of taking the Bar Exam." Defense Counsel advised.

"Commissioners of the court, the subject identified as Tyrone Brady sold one twelve-ounce bottle of beer labeled Corona to a minor without requesting proof of age. The minor, identified as a witness for the State was equipped with a valid Ohio Identification card and accompanied by an undercover officer who witnessed the transaction. The attending officer will testify to the events of said transaction and validate the integrity of the violation." Prosecuting Counsel opposed.

Concluding statements from both prosecuting and defense counsel, the courtroom became silent as the commissioners deliberated upon presented arguments. Several minutes seemed like an hour had elapsed before the Commissioners re-addressed the courtroom.

"Counselors of this courtroom, it is the decision of the commission to dismiss the charges due to lack of evidence presented. Upon our review, we found no hard evidence to sustain the listed charges. A recording of the transaction would have brought certainty to this violation. However, testimony alone from the witnesses is circumstantial at best," affirmed Commissioner Gordon.

An awe of disappointment spread across the courtroom as the prosecution tried to rebuttal the commissioner's findings.

"Order, Order in the Court. Bailiff, please clear the court. Our session is now adjourned."

The defense counsel was elated from the Commissioner's decision. The bailiff continued clearing the courtroom as the prosecuting counsel left in anguish.

"This is some bullshit, public corruption in plain sight," murmured the investigating officer.

Back at the ODI Field Office, Jordan was typing up his case notes from their investigation. Detective Carter was standing at Jordan's desk pondering possible outcomes of the current investigation. He then began to place his concerns onto Jordan.

"You think this Haitian prick will call soon," asked Carter.

"You know Carter; I wonder if we weren't previous partners, would you even know any black people." Jordan replied.

Jordan stared at Carter for a second and returned back to typing his notes.
Carter scoffed at Jordan's comment as he stared at the top of Jordan's head.

Carte replies, "You act as if I'm racist."

Jordan sighed and stopped typing to look at Carter again. "Nah, I don't think you're racist, just insensitive to people of color when opening your prehistoric mouth. You speak with no filter and exercise compartmental feelings when exerting your thoughts. Contrary to your actions, you're just a poor sap who doesn't know any better."

Carter clears his throat and rubs his forehead with a confused face. "Tell me how you really feel my friend," replied Carter.

"I'm sorry, but you need to adapt to today's times or suffer a discourteous complaint from a civilian who see otherwise." Jordan stated.

Carter became lost in thought as he pondered Jordan's comments. Suddenly, the ring tone of Jordan's undercover phone caught the attention of the two colleagues. Jordan reaches into his desk drawer to retrieve his cellphone.

"Who 'tis?" Jordan answers in a Trinidadian accent.

"Who 'tis? 'Tis be Johnnie B. I was told you were looking for me. For why, you seek me out?"

Jordan continued speaking in his Trinidadian cover and advised he was looking for a supplier with a good product of cocaine. Jordan noticed the skepticism in Johnnie B's voice during their call. He began thinking more of exercising his backup plan then going through with a meet. Jordan didn't want to spook his target, so he agreed to a sit down at the Juva De. Johnnie B instructed him to come by the club around 5 pm. He indicated the club would be closed to public, but open for business.

"Me number should of shown on your phone. Call tee number when you arrive and I'll buzz you up." Johnnie B instructed.

Jordan terminates the call and finds Carter looking at him with a curious face. He advises Carter it was Johnnie B on the line and a meet was in place for tonight.

"What do you need me to do?" Carter asked.

"Stay in the shadows and be my informational officer. I will feed you the details as they occur." Jordan instructed.

Carter didn't like being second fiddle to anyone, but he knew Jordan had his reasons on how he wanted to play this meet and he respected his request to shadow cover Jordan's moves. Agent Tyler then walks in on their conversation.

"Hey bro, what's up Carter? Tyler greets Jordan and Carter.

Jordan advised Tyler a meet has been arranged with Jonnie B for 5 p.m. today. He further indicated they were meeting at the Juva De. Tyler suggested they began going over details of their plan, leaving nothing to be questioned.

"You sure this shit will work," asked Carter.

Jordan scoffs with a smile as Tyler walks over to a nearby office closet. Tyler retrieves a few props from inside the closet. He then brings the them over to Jordan's desk.

"Here, use these props for your meet with Johnnie B. The cigars are made from Cuban leaves and Tribal tobacco. This unique blend gives a fragrance of marijuana. So, when you fire it up, it will smell like Weed and appear you're smoking a blunt," Explained Tyler.

Jordan nodded his head in agreement as he accepted the props for his cover. He was more concern on how he would make his intro with Johnnie B. Cater and Tyler continued fine tuning their strategy, looking for any hidden anomalies which might derail their plan.

The sun was starting to set, transitioning from a busy day into a mysterious night. Jordan looks down at his watch and it reads 5:05 p.m. The meet was set for 5 p.m., but Jordan didn't care of being late as he stood outside of the Juva De. He panned the area for possible counter intelligence before walking up to the entrance door. Jordan presses the buzzer to acknowledge his presence and seconds later, the door buzzes open. As he enters the establishment, Jordan is patted down by a security guard. The guard misses Jordan's weapon during his pat search and allows him to enter armed. Jordan walks over to the bar area where he's met by Johnnie B. The two men stood across from each another, only to be divided by the bar.

"Malik St. Charles, I presume." Johnnie B greeted.

"Johnnie-fucking-B." Jordan replied.

Johnnie B was a man of preciseness and hated to be kept waiting, especially if it involved business. He scolded Jordan about his tardiness for their meet.

"I no like 'tis first impression you show me. Why You late nigga?" Johnnie B inquired.

Jordan smugly replies, "Traffic, but please accept my apologies."

The two men chuckled at their comments as they stared at one another. Johnnie B snaps his finger and Carla walks over to the bar with a briefcase in hand.

"I believe you had interest in some sugar," asked Johnnie B?

"Yes, an eighth would pleasure my taste." Jordan replied.

Carla places the briefcase on the bar and slides it between Johnnie B and Jordan. Jordan gave an inquisitive look at Carla as he took possession of the case. Carla stared back like a watch dog when guarding its master.

 "My sugar is pure, that amount will cost you three bills for a taste." Johnnie B stated.

Jordan opens the briefcase to review its contents. He takes out a testing Kit to sample the integrity of Johnnie B's product. Jordan then places a small sample of product inside a testing tube and shakes it. The testing agent causes the cocaine to turns blue within seconds.

"Looks like we have a deal Bee," states Jordan.

Jordan closes the briefcase, only to find Johnnie B pointing a 44-Magnum at him. He swings the briefcase at Johnnie B's gun, deflecting its direction and causing it to fire a bullet into Carla's chest. After discharging his gun, Johnnie B flees through a back entrance of the bar and down a flight of stairs to a nearby exit. Carla lies on the bar floor, gasping for air and choking on her own blood. Jordan calls for an ambulance as he watches Carla pass away with her eyes open.

Seconds later into Johnnie B's escape, he's immediately abducted by unknown assailants as he exits the premises. In the mist of this altercation, Johnnie B drops his gun and is rendered unconscious by the assailants. They assailants then conceal Johnnie B's body into their trunk and drives off to an unknown location.

Meanwhile inside the Juva De, medical and police personnel are arriving on scene attending to Carla's death. Detective Carter takes over the scene, advising Crime Scene Investigators to begin processing. County Coroner personnel secure Carla's body onto a gurney after placing her into a body bag. She was then transported to the morgue for processing. Carter takes Jordan aside to ask what happen. Jordan explains Johnnie B shot Carla in his attempt to kill him. Carter tells Jordan he'll prepare a cover story to maintain the confidentially of their investigation. Jordan gives Carter a brotherly handshake, thanking him for handling the situation. He then exits the Juva De, while Carter stayed behind to supervise the collection of evidence.

CHAPTER NINE: FLY IN A SPIDER'S WEB

Johnnie B is awakened from water being thrown onto his body. He finds himself bonded to a chair with an old friend staring him in the face.

"Wakey, wakey nigga! Where da fuck is me money," asks Caribbean Jay?

Johnnie B was dazed and suffering from a mild concussion due to being knocked unconscious. He had blurred vision and unable to focus on Jay's voice. Jonnie B struggles to communicate back.

"What, what are you talking about?"   Johnnie B asks.

Caribbean Jay reminds him about the three kilos of coke he gave Johnnie B six months ago. Johnnie B's mouth began to twitch with a nervous smile, because he remembered the drugs were given on consignment and never paid back. Jay strikes Johnnie B, knocking him unconscious again. Fifteen minutes later Johnnie B awakens. This time, Caribbean Jay is accompanied by Jordan (Malik).

"It's about time your bitch-ass woke up! Tis nigga, chuckled Jordan.

Jordan continued with taunting comments, placing fear into the bonded Johnnie B and making him feel like a fly caught in a spider's web. He thought his life was over when Jordan reminded Johnnie, he tried to kill him. In this line of work, a failed attempt on a man's life brings forth an automatic death wish.

 "You tried to kill me, but it was your bitch who got dead. So now, your life belongs to me. I want your connect and their suppliers. And maybe I won't let Jay kill you for the money you owe him. It's the only way your black ass going to live nigga. Which in terms going to make you my bitch!"   Jordan stated.

Johnnie B was at the mercy of his adversaries.   He knew the only way to survive was to agree with the presented terms. He looks at Caribbean Jay and then pans to Jordan.

"Ok, ok, I'll do it. Whatever you need me to do, I will do it," exclaims Johnnie B.

Jordan smiles at Johnnie B's submission. However, Caribbean Jay wasn't satisfied. Knowing that Johnnie B owed him money from a previous agreement, He had other plans for him.

The next morning, sounds of a vibrating cellphone rings out while Jordan lay sleeping. His eyes flutter as they slowly open to the echoing noise. Jordan began searching for his phone and finds it under a pillow next to him. He answers the call, learning its Agent Tyler on the other end.

"Bro, where have you been? I haven't heard from you in a couple of days. Is everything good with you?" Tyler asks.

Jordan stated to have been clearing his head from the shooting at the Juva De. Tyler being a former Navy SEAL and now government agent, since something more to Jordan's story. He requested they meet later in the afternoon. Jordan agreed and instructed Tyler to meet him at "Chicken Shack".

Three hours had past and a mist of rain had overcast the city. The church of Saint Terry's we're in progress, conducting small group sessions with its members. Father Terry stood before his congregation as the overseer of this spiritual gathering.

"Members of Saint Terry, I stand before you as your guide for any questions pondering you. These small groups are created as a channel to release all uncertainty troubling your eternal soul. Now each group will have a leader and a person to scribe all commentaries. Thirty minutes from now, each leader will present their groups discussions and I will address them before the congregation. Please begin!" Terry instructed.

Indistinctive chatter began to immerse from the gathered groups as they begin discussing matters of interests. Father Terry was watching over his members when a clergyman approached his side.

"Excuse me Father, but you have someone who wishes to speak with you."

Father Terry looks over the clergyman's shoulder and sees Jaden Kraus waiting in the boundaries of the church. He acknowledged Jaden's presences and nods for him to meet in a nearby office.

Minutes later in the church's executive office, Father Terry and Jaden sat down before each other. Terry was a man of the cloth, but he scowled to unscheduled visits from colleagues of illicit business.

"This better be good," stated Father Terry.

Jaden scoffed at Terry's temperament.   He hated conducting business at his church, just as much as Terry disliked impromptu visits. Jaden senses the dislike off of Terry and wanted nothing more than to be somewhere else. However, business had to be conducted and the place of conversation was never his choice.

"Matters of operations have halted in the Harvard area. It appears Lady Carla has gotten herself dead and Johnnie B is nowhere to be found. Word on the street indicates some Trinidadian Cat is in the middle of this debacle. Have you heard about this?" Jaden stated.

Placing the left index finger across his lips and pondering thoughts before speaking, Father Terry answers Jaden's question.

"I'm a fucking Priest! What might I know about some dead nigger-bitch and a Haitian immigrant, let alone some Trini who's beefing with them all? My concerns are in the laundry business. Which reminds me, your dads' laundry is ready. Tell him I've already took my cut off the top. Should I come across information on your associates, I'll be sure to let you know. Now, if you would excuse me, I need to get back to the congregation. You can take your father's money as you exit's the side entrance. And Jaden, be quick about it. I need you not to be a spectacle at my church."

Father Terry stands up from their conversation, awaiting Jaden to do the same. Jaden slowed in rising from his seated position and casually walked over to the table possessing two duffle bags.   He gathered the bags containing his father's laundered money and paused in thought before removing them. As he stood by the table, he casts another question to Father Terry.

"Are you sure your eyes on the street haven't seen Johnnie B? Jaden asks.

Father Terry replies, "My position is only about the money, I leave the politics to you gangsters."

Jaden smiles and then exits through the side door of Father Terry's office. Terry returns to his congregation to pastor the spiritual groups.

Currently, inside the Chicken Shack was Jordan sitting at a table drinking his soda. He observes Tyler to walk in shaking the rain from his clothing. Jordan acknowledges his presence and invites him over to where he sat. A waitress walks over to their table as Tyler is sitting down.

"May I take your order gentlemen?" The waitress asks.

Jordan takes the liberty to order for the both of them, while Tyler smiles at the waitress "Coke" bottle figure and round ass.

"We'll take two Polish boys and two grape sodas." Jordan responded.

Tyler continues smiling at the waitress as she walks away. Jordan clears his throat to get his attention. Tyler turns his head back around to face Jordan and engage into conversation.

"Since the shooting at the club you've been dark. What's up with that," stated Tyler.

Jordan tells Tyler how his nephew and an associate snatched Johnnie B off the streets the other night. It was Caribbean Jay and a "Zoe Pound" member who subdued Johnnie B as he fled the scene after shooting Carla. Tyler asked Jordan did they still had him accosted. Jordan shook his head indicating "no". Jordan did advise he convinced Johnnie B to become their CI on any drug movement in the city.

Tyler suggested keeping him off-books for plausible deniability purposes. Suddenly, Jordan's cellphone began vibrating. The caller ID screen displays a call from Chief Jenkins. Jordan gets up from the table to have privacy during his call.

"Hey, I have to take this. It's Jenkins from CPD!

Tyler takes out his phone to check his text messages. He taps on an unread message from Agent Ford and began reading her text.

"Our CI from The Mirage indicates a large shipment of dope coming into the city within the next forty-eight (48) hours. Call me!"

The text from Ford was sent two hours earlier prior to Tyler's meeting with Jordan. Tyler began dialing Ford's phone, but it rang to voicemail. He leaves a message advising her to call him back. At this time, Jordan returns to the table concluding his call. Noticing Tyler had a pensive look on his face.

"What's was on your mind, bro?" Jordan asks.

"Ford text me indicating her CI had information on a drug shipment." Tyler replied.

"That's good news bro, but why so deep in thought?" Jordan asked.

"I'm not sure, bro. I have mix feelings about her CI," replied Tyler.

Jordan reminded his partner to always trust his gut when uncertainty arises. Just as Jordan was finishing his comment, the waitress returns with their orders and the two colleagues began enjoying their lunch.

Meanwhile at the House of Joe's funeral home, the mortician preps Carla's body to be embalmed. He attaches a clear tube onto a needle and then inserts it into Carla's right carotid artery. The mortician turns on his machine and allows it to push fluids through the tube, which then flushes Carla's blood out of a nearby vein. Her skin begins to turn a pinkish tone during the embalming process.

Minutes later, Johnnie B enters the funeral home undetected and makes his way to the embalming room. He watches in silence from a distance, not revealing his presence to the mortician. Johnnie B listens as the mortician talks to Carla as if she was still alive.

"My poor child, you were too young to leave this world. It seems like yesterday as I watched you play as a kid, and now I must say good bye to my only niece. No worries, your Uncle Joe will make sure you're look good for the viewing."

Joe became startled when he heard a crackling noise from a distance. He turns to locate its origin, squinting his eyes to see what lies in the near shadows of the embalming room. He questions the presence of the unknown.
"Hello, who's there," called out Joe.

"No worries old man. I'm not here to hurt you." Johnnie B stated.

Johnnie B steps from the shadows, displaying his presence to Joe. Joe turns off the machine to faced his uninvited guest and learns why he's in his embalming room.

"Who might you be?" Joe asks.

"I'm a friend of the family, a friend to your belated niece. We worked together at the Juva De", explained Johnnie B.

Joe turn back to attend his niece's embalming. He then scoffed at the comment of Johnnie B and his niece working together. Johnnie B could tell Joe wasn't pleased of his presence.

"My niece was never good with choosing men." Joe stated.

Johnnie B sucks his teeth, asking what Joe meant by his comment. Joe ignored Johnnie B's question and continued embalming his niece. Johnnie B became irritated with Joe dismissing the idea of his niece being associated him.

"You know old man; she was the only family I had in this fucked up city. She understood me. She was someone I could trust." Johnnie B exclaims.

Joe paused for a moment and then stated, "You always hurt the ones you trust?"

"What are you saying old man? You think she's dead because of me?" Johnnie B asks in a scowled voice.

Joe rubbed his tongue across his bottom teeth and gums, spitting remnants from his mouth. He then replies, "That's exactly what I'm saying. Look nigga, I'm old school Mason. I hear a lot of shit and I know a lot of shit. And the word on the street is, you got my niece dead by dealing with some Trinidadian mother-fucker. Due to the fact I'm not sure how true that is, I'll give you an out. But if I catch your ass around here again, it will be you on this table. Now say your goodbyes to my niece and get the fuck out." Joe disrobed his embalming apron and walked into the funeral parlor, leaving Johnnie B to say his goodbyes to Carla's body.

As the afternoon transition into the evening, Jaden arrives at Kraus' Gentlemen's Club. Kraus is in his office going over book keeping. Kraus looked over at his son and noticed the black duffel bags he'd left with Father Terry. Jaden smiles as he sat the bags on his father's desk.

"What's up Pop." Jaden greeted.

"I see the good Father entrusted you with my returns." Kraus stated.

"Why wouldn't he, I am your blood." Jaden replied.

Kraus chuckled with a deviant smirk and replied, "It Doesn't mean I want kill you if you'd lost my money."

Jaden pondered his dad's comment, wondering if he'd kill him over a mistake. Although Kraus was a ruthless piece of shit, he wouldn't kill his only child. He wanted to make a point to his son about business-sense and accountability to conduct. Jaden took his dad's direction seriously, due to the line of business they conducted. He knew at any time their lives could end from a bad decision.

Jaden took a seat at his father's desk. Kraus paused from editing his books and engaged his son's attention, sensing Jaden wanted to talk.

"Did my comment catch your attention?" Kraus asks.

Kraus wanted to be sure he had Jaden's undivided attention. Jaden nodded his head to acknowledge his father he did. Kraus then placed his elbows upon the desk and clasp his hands together. He cleared his throat, to assure his voice wouldn't crack when speaking to Jaden.

"Good! You're my only child and I introduced you to the game at an early age. When your mom died, I had to take care of you the best way I knew how. All this you see here, is for you to take when I'm gone." Kraus explained.

"What if I'm not ready? You're the only family I have!" Jaden exclaimed.

Kraus sighs as he tries to explain the endgame to their way of life. "Son, it's not if, but when our tickets are punched. Being a cop in this city allowed me to see various ways of living. I just got tired of living on the fence and made a stand for what I believed in. One day you'll do the same, and I hope your choice will be better than mine. Just know, mistakes will kill you and the next man may not give you the opportunity for an explanation."

Jaden felt his cellphone vibrating. He takes it out to see a text from Father Terry. Jaden scoffs at the message as he read it.

"One of my eyes on the street saw Johnnie B leaving House of Joe's funeral home. It appears your ghost has risen." Text reads.

As Jaden places his phone away, Kraus observes him pondering the message. Having respect for Jaden's privacy, Kraus didn't want to ask who text him. However, his fatherly instinct compelled him to do so.

"Who was that," asked Kraus.

Jaden indicated it was no one important. Kraus smiles at his son's comment. He knew Father Terry had his hooks into him and Jaden couldn't shake his existence. Kraus continued giving Jaden more advice about the enemy being camouflage.

"Beware of the cloth. For the person who wears it may not have your best interest." Kraus indicated.

Jaden nodded in acknowledgment of his father's comment. He then greeted his father goodbye as he left his office. Kraus knew Jaden was a man of his own decisions and no matter what he said about Father Terry, he knew his son must make his own choices.

The sun began to set as the evening grew older, bringing nightfall over the City of Cleveland. Johnnie B enters his apartment to be greeted by an uninvited guest. He could only see the subject's silhouette as his voice projected from a chair. Johnnie B began to experience a melancholy feeling while facing a person he couldn't see. The subject then turns a nearby lamp to unveil his identity.

"It's about time you came home." Guest stated.

"Jaden, what the fuck are you doing in my apartment?" Johnnie B asked.

"It is I who should be asking the questions mother-fucker. Where the fuck you've been and why is Carla dead?" Jaden stated.

Johnnie B stuttered in his attempt to rebuttal Jaden's question, but Jaden quickly cuts him off and continue his attack of questioning. Johnnie B felt in fear of his life due to the uncertainty of Jaden's character.
"To think you were dead too, but I've should have known a sneaky bastard like you would slip death. So, how did she die Bee?" Jaden asked.

Johnnie B chose his words carefully before answering Jaden. "Carla set up a buy for me. The guy seemed like a mark, but I misjudged his character."

Jaden wanted so much to kill Johnnie for Carla's death, but he needed him alive to   keep his business with Father Terry flowing.

"You and I have some business to conduct. For now, no transactions without my approval. The Trini-Nigga' may not be who he says he is. Stay close, I'll be in touch on the re-up." Jaden instructed as he exited the apartment.

Johnnie B thought to himself, "How the fuck 'tis nigga got past my alarm system?" He then sits down in the chair where Jaden sat, pondering their conversation. Five minutes later, a knock came upon his door. Thinking to himself it was Jaden returning, but to his surprised it was Caribbean Jay standing at his door.

"Ta' looks upon your face, tells me you were expecting someone else. Me wonder who that be," chuckled Caribbean Jay.

Johnnie stood aside so Caribbean Jay could walk into his apartment. He then watched Jay take a blunt from inside his jacket and a lighter from his outside pocket. Jay intended to light his blunt, but was quickly interrupted by Johnnie B.

"Wo, wo, wo! Take that shit to the balcony." Johnnie B shouts.

"Tis nigga!" Caribbean Jay chuckles as he walks onto the balcony.

Before closing the door, Johnnie looks into the hallway for Jaden's presence. He was curious as to how fast he'd disappeared prior to Jay's arrival. Unable to locate him, he then closes the door and joins Jay on his balcony.

"Why are you here Jay?" Johnnie B asked. He stood left of Jay as they both looks onto the night life of Cleveland.

"Your balcony gives a great view of the city mon. Peaceful, appreciative, everything you need to relax your mind and let your conscious be free." Caribbean Jay stated.

Caribbean Jay inhales a large amount of smoke from his blunt and blows it into the night air. He passes the blunt to Johnnie B and continues to talk. "I don't understand mon', I gave you one job to do and simple instructions to follow. Set up shop in Cleveland, flip my dope and return my money from consignment. Can you tell me, why I don't have me money?

Johnnie B clears his throat and replies, "HHK and Jaden Kraus."

Caribbean Jay glanced at Johnnie B from his peripheral and said, "Nigga I should kill you dead and throw your remains off this balcony."

Fearing Caribbean Jay may act on his words, Johnnie B pleaded why he sided with Jaden. "I know you're upset and things, but I was at me wits end for help. HHK offered protection while I sold your dope."

"My dope is why you should've come to me. These niggas aren't Zoe Pound. They can't protect shit, let alone you!" Caribbean Jay stated.

Caribbean Jay then switched his temperament and got back into business mode. Jay wanted his money from the dope he gave Johnnie B months ago. He knew killing him wouldn't generate any funds. Johnnie B had to remain alive to recoup revenue on his investment.

"Word on the streets indicates a big shipment of dope coming in. Find out where and let me know. This will be your way to make things right with me. I'll be in touch." Caribbean Jay stated.

Caribbean Jay then exits the balcony and Johnnie B's apartment, leaving him to ponder their conversation. Feeling trapped like a fly in a spider's web, Johnnie B had to incur a plan fast. He didn't want to find himself on Joe's embalming table.

It was twelve midnight and Agent Ford is meeting with her CI from the Mirage Night Club. The two are sitting at a table by the boating docks. As they're talking, Agents Tyler and Jordan walks up to join them.

"Hope we're not too late for the party?" Tyler stated.

Jordan sits next to Ford's CI as she continues debriefing him. The CI indicated a snowfall of dope coming in by boat. Tyler and Jordan listen in as the details unfold. Ford was sketching notes for a possible timeline and date of delivery.

"The location for the drop has not been set. All interested parties will be made aware on the day of arrival," stated the CI.

"When will that date be?" Ford asked.

"Before next Friday! The distributors want its product on the streets by Columbus Day Weekend. A lot of celebs in town during that time." CI stated.

The CI then apologizes for not having conclusive information but promises to advise when the product arrives. He then gets up from their meet and enters the club to complete his shift. Agents Ford, Tyler and Jordan deliberate on a pre-tactical plan before advising the rest of their team.

Meanwhile at Saint Terry's Catholic Church, Father Terry is meeting with Kraus. Kraus was dropping off more illicit funds to be washed through church tithes. The two men were going over financial returns from their illicit activity. Suddenly, a startling noise caught their attention. They immediately stop conversing to investigate.

"I thought you said we were the only one here." Kraus stated.

Father Terry immediately exited his office to investigate the suspicious noise. As he and Kraus entered the hallway, they observed a shadow figure running towards the sanctuary. Kraus took off into a full sprint after the subject. He closed the distance between them very quickly as the chase ended in the sanctuary. Kraus punched the subject in his face, causing him to fall upon the sanctuary floor. He then rolled the subject over to identify him as a homeless person. Father Terry arrives to their location as Kraus starts to question the homeless man. Placing his knee was on the subject's chest, Kraus sticks his gun into the man's mouth.

"No need for that, put your gun away you idiot!" Terry shouted.

"He May have heard something," stated Kraus.

"So, if he did, he couldn't tell anyone because he has no tongue. Now let him up. He seeks shelter here and is allowed inside this church." Terry stated.

Kraus pulled the homeless man to his feet and apologizes for the incident at hand. The homeless man walks over towards a nearby pew and makes a pad for the night. Kraus and Terry exit the sanctuary, continuing their conversation in the hallway of the church.

"That Fart-nugget almost got himself shot." Kraus boasted.

"Be not worried, for his spirit is more stilled then yours. His accounts will not conflict with ours," explains Terry.

Kraus stares at Father Terry as he goes into a detail explanation of why the homeless man is very loyal.

"You know the difference between you and I" asked Terry.

"No!" Kraus answered.

"My money laundering helps you stay clean and legit. Your money help pay for revisions to this church. This church gives sanctuary to all of us. I look at things in a multi-dimensional plane, while you continuously think one dimensional. Your acts are of contemporary human behavior.

A theory derived from perspective social workers. If you want to survive in the game we play, you will need to advance your dynamics and broaden your ecological perspective. It's the only way to avoid social isolation. And trust me, you don't want to be isolated my friend." Terry exclaims.

Kraus chuckled and says, "You assume I would be motivated by your short sermon, but I just want to make money. Make sure mine is ready for pick up on our next visit." Kraus ends their conversation and exits the church.

It's five o 'clock in the morning. Street dealers are trying to make theirs bones by flipping product on the corner of Charles and Euclid Avenue. Back in the eighties, this area lived middle-class blacks with money and some of them had million-dollar homes. Since the corruption and political scandals from City Council members, the area is now called the corner. A dispensary location for drugs and illicit activities. Detective Carter is sitting in an unmarked police vehicle conducting surveillance. He observed a young black male exits the corner store counting unknown items in his left palm with his right index finger. The inadvertent gesture usually signifies a drug dealer counting his product before sales. In the middle of his visual audit, a black female engages the observed target with conversation. Carter descends his passenger window and points a small microphone in their direction. He wanted to capture their conversation for intelligence gathering.

"Hey daddy, what you got for me?" The black female asks.

The male target replies, "I have some Tic-Tac's. You need some?"

"I'm looking for that good candy, some white sugar if you have it. Can you spare a neighbor a cup?" The black female asked.

"I'm out of sugar right now. I got to hit the store in a couple of days. Get with me then or have some Tic-Tac's now." The male target says.

"I'll hit you up later, those tic-tac's aren't going to satisfy this sweet tooth," says the black female.

She departs company, leaving the black male to seek sales from another customer. Carter made note of this interaction and then drove off to his next location.

Later that morning Jordan is headed to the ODI field office. He's suddenly yielded by an unmarked vehicle at the intersection of 9th Street and Euclid Avenue. Jordan pulls his vehicle aside in compliance to the traffic stop. He then noticed a familiar figure exiting the vehicle.

"Strange meeting you here." Jordan stated.

"I didn't want to bring adverse attention to you. You appear to be undercover," says Chief Jenkins.

"Well Chief, even a simple traffic stops draws that attention." Jordan replied.

"I apologize! it seems you've evolved well to this cloak and dagger shit." Chief Jenkins chuckled.

"Even So Chief, I won't forget what you've taught me. So, what's on your mind?" Jordan asked.

The Chief indicated his narcotic detectives came across information about a drug shipment. He then asked Jordan did he have any intelligence about the incoming dope. Jordan advised the Chief he did not but would keep him in the loop should he hear something. Jenkins smiled and said his goodbyes, allowing Jordan to get on with his morning. Jordan then drives off in route to his briefing at ODI.

Fifteen minutes later, Jordan arrives at the ODI Field Office. He greets everyone upon entering the briefing room. Detective Carter is in attendance as for he was invited by Agent Ford.

"Team, usually I start off the briefing with updates of my own and then turn it over to someone else. Today, I'm going to let Detective Carter start off with his intelligence." Ford stated.

 Carter stands up and thanks Ford for the opening remarks. He then breaks into his briefing to the attending agents. "Early hours of this morning, I was at the location of Charles Street and Euclid Avenue gathering intelligence. Upon doing so, I observed a young dealer and a potential customer engage in conversation. I was able to retrieve dialogue via a directional microphone." Detective Carter takes out a micro cassette tape and places it inside a playing device, which played the captured conversation.

[Female voice]: Hey daddy, what you got for me?"

[Male voice]: I have some Tic-Tac's. You need some?"

[Female voice]: I'm looking for that good candy, some white sugar if you have it."

Carter stops the tape and speeds it up to the important part relative to their on-going investigation. He then presses play for continuation of the tape.

[Male voice]: I'm out of sugar right now. I got to hit the store in a couple of days. Get with me then or have some Tic-Tac's now."

[Female voice]: I'll hit you up later, those Tic-Tac's aren't going to satisfy this sweet tooth."

"I believed this information may be related to our suspected shipment coming in soon." Carter stated.

Agent Ford interjects to bring relevance of Carter's intelligence. She indicates his intelligence confirms her CI's information about the suspected drug shipment to hit the city in a few days.

"My CI indicates suspected drug distributors want their product on the streets before Columbus Day weekend. Which means, we only have a couple of days to find out where these drugs are being held." Ford stated.

Jordan indicated the Chief of CPD stated their narcotics unit had intelligence of drugs coming in as well. Carter seemed jealous that Jenkins came to Jordan instead of him. Ford reminded the rivals to get back on task. She then continued with her directives to the agents.

"You guys hit up your CI's hard for info and find these drugs before they find every street corner of our city." Ford concluded.

Indistinctive chatter began immersing within the duty room as Agent Ford adjourns her briefing. Jordan looks over at Agent Tyler. They both gave each other the nod as an indication to get to work ASAP. Agent Duncan observes her colleagues, wondering what they were plotting. Stanzell was busy going over his field notes, while Ford and Carter conversated.

It was 12:30 p.m., Jaden walks upon a street dealer posted in a bus stop. He demands a money count from his employee. The dealer handed Jaden a wad of cash and he took count of the given funds. The dealers eyes widen in fear when Jaden eyeballs him with a killer stare.

"Nigga, this shit is light! Where's the rest of my money?" Jaden demanded.

"My bag Jay, but there's been no customers. Shit is scarce right now." The dealer stutters with his reply.

Jaden chuckled as he addresses the dealer's reply, "Scarce, your dumb ass can't even spell the word. You think I don't know you've been skimming off the top, trying to play me for a fool."

Jaden observes his dealer to shake in fear while being questioned. He ponders the thought of shooting him for dishonesty. As a small tear then runs down Jaden's face, he removes a baby Glock from his pants pocket and displays it in his right hand. "I'm sorry bro, but its business!" Jaden said. He then shoots the dealer and watches his body falls to the ground inside the bus stop. Jaden wipes the tear from his face as he stood over the dealer's body. He then fires two more shots into the dealer's face to make sure he's dead. Jaden sees oncoming people walking towards the bus stop. He flees the scene to prevent being identified.

A woman comments as she walks upon the deceases body. "Oh my God, he's dead. Someone calls the police. Call the police!" The woman screams out for help, drawing onlookers to her location.
The digital text on Jordan's G-Shock read 12:55 p.m. He was meeting his wife for lunch at the Sandwich Shop near downtown Cleveland.

Jordan enters the delicatessen and finds his wife sitting at a window table for two. "Is this seat taken," asked Jordan?

Pam displays a beautiful smile and invites her husband to sit down. "Amazing, you found time to squeeze me into your crime fighting schedule." She replied.

Jordan chuckled at his wife's comment. He then replies, "Who said I wasn't working while we're having lunch."

Pam gave an inquisitive stare, pondering whether her husband was serious or not. Just as Pam was about to ask Jordan a question, their waitress walks up.

"What can I get you guys?" The waitress asks.

Jordan ordered two waters, one coffee and a lemonade. "Can you give us a moment on our entrees." Jordan asks.

"Sure, I'll be back in a moment, replied the waitress.

Jordan turns his attention back to his wife to entertain her question. "You were about to ask me a question before the interruption." Jordan stated.

Pam grinned and replied, "Indeed I was. Are we having a business meeting? Because I can charge this to the University if we are?"

As the couple engaged deep conversation, a slow passing Cadillac fires bullets into the establishment. Glass debris ricochets throughout the premises, causing Jordan to pull his wife to the floor. As bodies collapsed around him, Jordan could only think of his wife's safety. Suddenly, he snaps into combat mode and exits the establishment to engage the vehicle. Removing his Glock 27 from conceal carry, Jordan open fire onto the fleeing vehicle. The vehicle escapes with minor damages, limited to a few bullet holes and a shattered back window. Several black and white CPD units began arriving on scene due to the violent incident. The officers shouted commands at Jordan as they exited their vehicles. Jordan complies with the officer's commands. He then identifies himself as law enforcement.

"What happened here," asked one uniform officer's?

"My wife and I were having lunch inside when this unknown vehicle drove by dispensing bullets into the premises. There are a few casualties inside." Jordan stated.

Suddenly, a black Dodge Intrepid with red and blues lights displaying arrived on scene. It was Agent Tyler coming to his partners rescue. Tyler approached the yellow tape area where Jordan and his wife stood.

"Excuse me sir, who are you," questioned a uniform officer.

"Agent Tyler, ODI. This man you're questioning is my partner." Tyler stated.

Jordan and Tyler observed a confused look upon the officer's face. Jordan requested the officer to contact Detective Carter from Homicide. As soon as Jordan said that, Detective Carter was arriving on scene.

"What the hell," asked Carter?

"Drive-by with multiple victims inside. My wife and I are witnesses to the incident. I also captured the vehicles plate, H-H-K-4-L-F." Jordan explains.

Carter's eyes widen, for he remembered the same vehicle registration from the Juva De shooting involving Investigator Miller's death. It appeared a web of bodies were starting to link to all of Carter's cases.

"Let's get an inventory of names from inside and see why this place was marked as a target," instructed Carter.

Tyler goes inside to question witnesses, while Jordan and his wife gave their statements to Carter. Tyler began observing the carnage of dead bodies inside the sandwich shop, followed by a plethora of bullet holes in the store structure. He further counted eight casualties and three wounded. Tyler then found two employees not injured who witnessed the incident. They were crouched behind the counter for safe refuge. The store keepers told Tyler they heard breaking glass and patrons screaming as they took refuge. One of the employees indicated she witnessed the bodies of customers falling to the floor. She then states to have observed Jordan exit the deli with his gun in hand and fire his weapon at someone or something. She couldn't explain who Jordan was shooting at due to her hiding behind the counter. Concluding the witness' statements, Tyler walked outside of the premises to report his findings to Detective Carter.

As Tyler approached Carter, Jordan was explaining the direction in which the vehicle fled. Carter relayed Jordan's accordance to CPD dispatch in efforts to secure a chopper for search of the vehicle. Dispatch indicated there were no chopper's available at this time. Pam, distraught by what had occurred, stood in the background receiving medical attention. In the mist of this chaos, a mystery person was taking photos of Jordan and his colleagues. The Unsub then started taking several photos of Pam as she stood alone from the group. His position was concealed to prevent unwarranted attention.

Ford accompanied by Duncan and Stanzell arrived on scene after being called out by Tyler. They see the carnage of several dead and injured by-standers.

"Y-o-o-o, what the fuck happened here?" Stanzell asked.

"Dude, you're so extra," commented Duncan.

"Let's stay focused. Follow up with Tyler and see what we're working with! Ford instructed. She then walks over to Jordan to learn how her rookie agent was doing

"You injured?" Ford asked Jordan.

"I'm good, just my ego is bruised." stated Jordan.

  Her concerns of Jordan caught the attention of his wife. Pam felt like an outsider to the ODI family. She knew nothing of their daily survival as agents.
Detective Carter began studying the scene, dissecting the elements leading up to its crime. He didn't believe in coincidences, so he had to learn why the same black Cadillac from Miller's homicide was now linked to this crime scene.

"H-H-K-4-L-F," cited Carter as he wrote the registration on his notepad. He then retrieves his police radio from his waist area and contacted CPD dispatch.

"Central, this is John-Sam-9." Carter calls out.

"John-Sam-9, go ahead," replied Central Dispatch.

"Run Ohio Registration, Henry-Henry-King-four-Lincoln-Frank," requested Carter.

"Stand-by," replied dispatch.

Several minutes later, dispatch returns with information for Carter. "John-Sam-9, the listed registration is returning as nothing in file."

"Roger that," responded Carter.

Carter ponders the received information and states to himself, "Why would a civilian vehicle have cold plates as their registration? Could this be a government vehicle and if so, why is it involved with a homicide shooting?"
Carter's unanswered questions were eating at him and he needed clarity ASAP. "Guys, I'm going to check on a lead. I'll get back with you later!" Carter stated.

"Keep us posted on what you find!" Ford instructed.

The rest of the team acknowledges Carter's departure as he speeds off the scene. Jordan made a mental note to contact Carter as soon as he could. His abrupt departure appeared suspicious to him.

Later that evening, Pam fell asleep early after taking a sedative. She tossed and turned the entire night. Pam dreamt of the shooting over and over throughout the night. One segment of her dream envisioned Jordan being shot and Pam watching him die in her arms. She immediately wakes up in a cold sweat, looking for her husband. Pam noticed Jordan wasn't in bed, so she gets up to investigate his whereabouts. Pam walks downstairs to the kitchen area and sees a note on the island.

"Babe, I didn't want to wake you. You look so peaceful in your slumber. Besides, I figured you needed your rest due to your tossing and turning throughout the night. I took the liberty to make a small breakfast for you. Peek inside the microwave, where you will find eggs and bacon. Love you!"   Jordan wrote.

Pam smiles at her note and whispers to herself, "I love you too baby."

After eating her breakfast, showering and getting dressed for her daily events; Pam felt rejuvenated. She was still shaken from the shooting the day before and its affects placed Pam's senses on high alert. She went through every room of their home to make sure all was secured. "Am I being paranoid," she said aloud. As Pam exited their two-car garage in her candy-apple-red Mercedes, she saw a black sedan, with tinted windows, pull away. Pam was unable to make out the vehicle description but had intentions of calling her husband to advise him. As she was beginning to dial Jordan's cell, Pam noticed her neighbor, Mr. Crawley. The elderly gentleman was waving his arms up and down, trying to capture her attention. Pam pulled to the end of their driveway and rolled her passenger-side window down. Crawley places his head through Pam's window.

"My Dear child, that vehicle had been sitting in front of your house all morning. It arrived shortly after Jordan left. I was sitting on the porch enjoying my coffee and reading the news when it arrived. At first, I thought the Cunningham's across from you were expecting visitors, then I remembered they're on vacation for the week. Whomever was inside stayed parked for two hours, prior to you exiting your garage." Mr. Crawley exclaims.

Pam took note of what Crawley said. She made him promise to keep an eye on her house and to call the police if the vehicle return.

"No worries, I'll just call Jordan myself should that vehicle return. He's the only police I trust around here," stated Crawley.

Pam chuckled at her neighbor's enthusiasm. As she departed his company and pulled her vehicle onto the street, Pam checked her rear-view mirror for any stationary vehicles with intentions of following her. Troubled from the shooting a day before and unable to secure a description of today's vehicle, made Pam feel uneasy about everything.

She had no idea who was in the black sedan and didn't want to find out no time soon. Pam continues driving, checking her mirror to see if she's being followed. Upon coming to a red light which halted her travels, her cellphone ranged with the "Atomic-Dog" ringtone. It was her cousin "Miles". "What's up, Cuzzo?" Pam asked.

"I'm playing hooky from work because I want to spend time with you," stated Miles.

"I call bullshit," replied Pam.

The traffic light turns green and Pam becomes mobile again. As she travels through traffic, the conversation with Miles continues. Miles adjusts his tone for a more direct approach. He knew Pam had no patience for a fluff conversation.

"Look, I don't want to discuss this over the phone." Miles explained.

"Ok, where would you like to meet," asked Pam?

"Coventry Gym! We can get in a game of racket ball while we talk," stated Miles.

Pam chuckled and replied, "Well, lucky for you I have my gym bag in the trunk. I don't mind kicking your butt in a couple of games."

Miles chuckled back and stated, "You wish, I'll see you in thirty. Chow!"

Pam's terminates the call and reroutes her destination for Coventry Gym. Her impulse decision to meet Miles erased her intentions to call Jordan about the suspicious vehicle. Currently at a local McDonald's, Agents Tyler and Jordan meet up with Caribbean Jay. The party of three sat in a secluded booth away from other patrons.

"What up, Unc," greeted Jay.

"Is this who I think it is?" Tyler asked.

"In the flesh, my Zoe Pound-nephew," stated Jordan.

"No shit, this little nigga is a legend of Court TV," said Tyler.

Jay chuckled at Tyler's comment. Although he had no love for the law, he respected Tyler's character. Stories from his uncle Jordan painted Tyler as a War Hero to Jay.   Jay began to inform Jordan and Tyler about a huge drug shipment coming into the city. He indicated Johnnie B will be holding the first portion of product at the Juva De. Jay further stated the other half of product will be stored at another location, unknown until he meets with Johnnie B tomorrow night.

"I only ask Unc, you to let me walk away with the product Johnnie B owes me?" Caribbean Jay requested.

Jordan looks over at Tyler for his approval. Tyler flashes a side glance at Jay and looks back at Jordan. He had no intentions of coming between any precursor arrangements between the two. Tyler then clears his throat and speaks on Jay's comment.

"I'm good with whatever. I just want the mother-fuckers who killed Mookie!"

Jay replies, "Rumor has it, some white-nigga name Kraus was behind the hit."

"What, you mean former CPD Kraus? The mother-fucker who owns Kraus' Gentlemen's Club?" Jordan asked.

Yeah, his bitch-ass son Jaden is the distributor for the Cleveland area. According to Johnnie B, Jaden has been fronting him protection while he sold his dope throughout night clubs in the city." Caribbean Jay explains.

Jordan looks at Tyler and says, "This shit ends tomorrow night. And I don't care how many toe tags we put on mother-fuckers to end it!"

Meanwhile at Coventry Gym, Pam is pulling into the parking lot. She finds an isolated parking spot close to the front entrance of the gym. Pam begins to text Jordan about the suspicious vehicle at their home, but is distracted again when Miles beeps his car horn. He then parks his vehicle next to Pam's.

"What up Cuzzo, glad you can make it." Miles greeted.

"Looks like someone is a little late," said Pam with a smile.

Pam and Miles grew up like brother and sister, instead of cousins. Pam exits her vehicle to grab her gym bag from the trunk. Miles stands alongside of her vehicle with his backpack on his left shoulder.

"Woman, I'm only a few minutes late. Besides, it's the first time I've ever known you to be on time. I always thought you would be late for your own funeral." Miles stated. The two laughs as they walk into the gym.

Twenty minutes later, Miles was sweatier than a farm goat on a hot day. It appeared Pam was more athletically inclined then Miles assumed. He was bent over gasping for air. Pam walks past him and gives a slap upon the buttocks with her racket.

"Tapped that ass, didn't I?" Pam celebrated in a joking voice.

"Damn girl, when did you get so good at racket ball?" Miles asked.

"It's all in the wrist, cuzzo!" Pam stated.

"Shit let's take a break," said Miles.

Miles retrieves a bottle of water from his gym bag. He then joins Pam as they sat on the court floor with their backs against the wall. Miles explains to Pam his real reason of wanting to meet with her. He heard info about a planned attack on a police officer's life. Miles became concerned when he learned the attack on her and Jordan.

"Cuzzo, you know I prepare taxes for the illicit clientele of Cleveland." Miles stated.

Pam nods her head in acknowledgement. Miles stated of overhearing information about a hit on a cop while preparing his clients quarterly taxes. He indicated talk of that nature was commonly presented. But during a particular conversation, the details caught his attention.

"You ever heard of the name Kraus?" Miles asked.

"No." Pam stated.

Miles continued to explain Kraus' illicit business operations and his connection with high ranking city officials. He further explained Kraus' son was a hire hand, sometimes employed by corrupted city officials to do their bidding. Miles indicated Jordan's name came up during the conversation, but was unsure in what tense used. He only heard bits and pieces due to poor ear hustling.

"Does Jaden drive a black sedan?" Pam asked.

"He drives a black Cadillac CTS." Miles stated.

Pam was starting to place the pieces together. The hit her cousin made reference to was targeted for Jordan. Pam immediately reached into her gym bag and retrieve her cellphone. She began dialing Jordan's cell, but was deferred to his voicemail. Pam tried again and again, but the same results occurred. She then leaves Jordan a voice message, requesting him to call her ASAP.

Pam became frantic. Miles could see his cousin's demeanor had abruptly changed. She began shaking from the information he told her. Miles tries to console Pam by embracing her with a hug.

In coincidental to their location, Chief Jenkins of CPD was enjoying a spa day at the same gym. He's currently sitting in the steam room with his eyes closed when an unannounced person enters. The unidentified male is dress in a cloth robe with a hood attached. The dense fog of steam and hooded robe, conceals the males face as he sits close to the Chief. The male then retrieves a syringe from his robe filled with a clear fluid. He then pricks the Chief's neck, inserting the fluid into his body. Jenkins eyes open and his body began convulsing, later leading to his death. The mystery male exits the steam room undetected.

Twenty minutes later, Pam and Miles are exiting the gym. They observe a variety of emergency vehicles in the parking lot. Pam looks over her shoulder and observes the Coroner's hauling a body from inside the gym. Miles turns to see what his cousin is looking at.

"What's going on over there?" Miles asked.

As Pam turns back around, she sees her husband and his partners walking towards them. He inquires of why Pam was at the gym instead of work.

"Babe, what are you doing here?" Jordan asks.

"Enjoying a workout with Miles," replied Pam.

"Hey Jordan." Miles greeted Jordan.

"What's up, Miles." Jordan greeted Miles.

Pam tried to inform Jordan of what Miles told her, but his attention was captured by the body being escorted from the gym. Jordan walks over to the gurney and pulled back the sheet. Carter and Tyler accompanied Jordan as he looks down at Jenkins lifeless body.

"How did he die," questioned Jordan?

The Coroner indicated possible heart failure but promised to have more details pending an autopsy. Jordan became overwhelmed with grief as his mentor was carted off. He didn't want Carter and Tyler see him grieving, so he held his emotions inside.

"The Chief never mention of having heart problems. I've known this man for years. He would have said something to me." Jordan exclaims.

"Bro, sometimes people don't share their darkest secrets," stated Tyler.

"That's bullshit! The Chief was healthy as a horse," added Carter.

Pam glances at her watch. She then walks over to Jordan and his friends. Pam needed to tell her husband of what she witnessed earlier and learned from her cousin Miles.

"Excuse me fellas, can you give me and my husband five minutes."

Jordan tells Carter and Tyler he would catch up with them in a moment. He and Pam walks over to her Mercedes to continue their conversation. Jordan could see the urgency upon Pam's face. He wanted to learn what was on her mind.

"S-o-o-o, what's so important babe?" Jordan asked.

Pam went into detail on how her day came about and why she was at the gym. She then told Jordan about the black sedan parked outside of their home and Mr. Crawley observing the vehicle being park for at least two hours.

"As I exited the garage, the vehicle sped off. Mr. Crawley said the vehicle arrived shortly after you left this morning." Pam stated.

"Did you notice any other vehicles outside the black sedan?" Jordan asked.

Pam indicated of seeing no other vehicles in addition to the black sedan. Jordan scowled upon hearing Pam's news. She then advised Jordan of what Miles told her. Jordan became curious about the information he received from Pam. He then instructed her to go home and wait for his arrival. Jordan rejoined Tyler and Carter, informing them of what his wife told him. Tyler immediately called his contact at the U.S. Marshal's office, requesting a protection detail for Pam.

By this time, Pam was on her way home as directed by Jordan. She then thought to stop at the store to grab a roast and some potatoes for tonight's dinner. Every few minutes during travel, she found herself checking the rear-view mirror for followers. Pam pulls into the parking lot of Dave's Market; she then checks her mirrors before exiting the vehicle. Pam quickly entered the market and fifteen minutes later, exited to enter her vehicle. She checked her mirrors again as she pulled off and headed home. Nearing the destination of home, Pam made a right turn onto her street. She then checks for suspicious vehicles in the vicinity of her home. Upon seeing none, Pam activates the garage door and enters her home.

Less than two hours later the aroma of broiled roast filled the Jordan's home. Pam was in the kitchen stirring the butter into her mash potatoes. She heard the garage door open and then close thereafter. Pam couldn't help but be a little on edge.

She yelled, "Jordan, Anybody there?"

"Yes, it's me babe." Jordan replied.

Pam was relieved to see it was her husband entering the kitchen from their garage. Jordan advised Pam he'd spoke with the Marshals outside of their house to confirm her protection detail. Pam seemed relieved from the news, but still had her reservations.

"We're good baby! The Marshals are good at what they do. Look, I have an undercover assignment taken place tomorrow night. Hopefully, we can tie things up with a bust and get all of this behind us." Jordan exclaimed.

 "I'll feel safe when there's no more protection detail and we can relax without worries," said Pam.

Jordan pours a glass of Cabernet Sauvignon for himself and another for Pam. The couple toasted and sat down for dinner.

Next morning at St. Terry's Catholic Church, Father Terry sat in his office going over the church's financial books. He glanced at the clock and it read ten o'clock in the morning. He realized Kraus hadn't called to schedule the pickup for his money. Terry grew curious as to why? He picked up the phone to call him, but got the sudden urge to call an adversary instead. Terry began dialing the digits of Commissioner Gordon's phone. The phone line ranged four times before Gordon answered. Terry greets the Commissioner in a sarcastic manner.

"Well, hello family." Terry greeted.

"You got balls to be calling me. We're not family anymore. That word comes as an insult to me." Gordan replied.

"Very well Commissioner, family we are not. I just thought we could bury the hatchet and become civil with one another." Terry stated.

In an angry voice, the Commissioner rants, "Civil we'll never be. You don't think the death of my daughter isn't by your hands.

Terry rebuttals, "I'm a man of the cloth, I don't give or take the life of others."

The Commissioner replies, "But your associates do, by your orders. Although I cannot prove it as of yet, but you will pay for your illicit deeds."

Commissioner Gordon terminates the call, leaving Terry chuckling on the other end. Terry then initiates another call, this time it was to Kraus. He wanted to know why his constituent hadn't called.

Meanwhile, Jordan was sitting at home eating a mid-morning snack. As he read the morning paper, he observed the headline "CPD Chief Found Dead in Gym." Sadden from the death of a close friend, Jordan places the newspaper down and reaches for the TV remote. He turns on the television set displaying a syndicated TV show. Not happy with the current selection, Jordan began flipping through channels to find something he'll like. He then hears his cellphone vibrating on the kitchen island. Jordan rises from the breakfast table and walks over to the island.

"Who this?" Jordan answered.

Jordan recognizes the voice to be Agent Tyler. He tells Jordan they have a briefing at 5:30pm. Jordan advises Tyler he would be there and then terminates his call. Pam is walking into the kitchen as Jordan utters his feelings aloud.

"This shit just got real!" Jordan stated.

"What shit, just got real?" Pam asked.

Jordan chuckled as he answered his wife's question. "That comment wasn't for you to hear. But since you did, I was referring to my assignment tonight."

Pam walked over to the Island where Jordan stood. She embraced her husband with a loving hug and stated, "Stay prayed up and come back to me in one piece."

  Jordan replies, "Roger that!" He then embraces his wife with the same hug and kisses her upon the forehead.

Later in the afternoon, Jordan exits his home and enters his undercover vehicle parked in the driveway. While sitting behind the wheel, he began preparing his mind for tonight's assignment. Jordan was a person who played scenarios throughout his mind to cover all possible outcomes. He then began thinking, "An outcome is no good without the blessing of the Lord." At that moment, Jordan's religion convinces him to seek God's approval before taking on his mission. He exits his driveway and traveled to Canaan Catholic Church for sanctuary. Several minutes later, Jordan arrives at the church parking lot. He looks down at his watch and it read 3:45p.m. Jordan exits his vehicle to enter the church. He later finds himself standing in the foyer, contemplating his entry of the sanctuary. The last time Jordan been inside this church is when Kim was alive. He takes a deep breath to calm his mind and spirit. Jordan continues the breathing exercises, until a feeling of calmness overtook his body.

Felling clear in mind and body, Jordan enters the sanctuary to kneel before the statue of Jesus. He further bows his head, exhibiting the position for several minutes in silence. Concluding his meditation, Jordan raises his head to ask the Lord for forgiveness. "Father in heaven, thank you for everything you've done for me. Let not my sins be the judgement of my soul. But forgive me of the negative events which may shine upon my life. For I'm only human and imperfect of being your child. Lead me not into temptation and protect me with your Shield of Buckler. As I fight upon my enemies whom try to take my life, let them not succeed in triumph of their fight. Lift me above them by placing their head at my feet. Amen!" Jordan rises to his feet, smiles at the statue and walks out of the church to enter his vehicle.

In continuing his travels, Jordan arrives at the office an hour before the briefing. He takes a seat at his desk and turns on the desktop computer. The time stamp on his computer reads 4:30pm. Ford is in her office, looking through a window overseeing the agent's duty room. Jordan's back is to her view. She then closes the blinds of her office and sits at her desk. Agent Ford began examining notes as preparation for the briefing. A stillness covers the agent's duty room, like a calm wind before a storm. As time elapsed, more and more agent's arrived for duty. The stillness transitioned into indistinctive chatter, bringing life to the duty room. Jordan looks up from his computer to observed Agents Stanzell and Duncan entering the duty room. He further pans the room in search of Tyler, but notice he hasn't arrived yet. Jordan smiles and gives a head gesture to acknowledge Duncan and Stanzell's arrival.

"Where's your boy?" Duncan referenced about Tyler.

"I have no idea. I assume he'll be here shortly, being its fifteen minutes until briefing," replied Jordan.

"R-I-g-h-t," stated Duncan as she smiled and walked over to her desk.

Jordan chuckled at her comment and went back to typing on his desktop.
Seconds after his encounter with Duncan, Jordan's cell began vibrating. He opens his flip phone to a text from Tyler.

"Meet me outside in the parking lot," read Tyler's text.

Jordan discreetly leaves his desk and exits the building. He finds Tyler and Detective Carter by his car.

"What's up bro, why the cloak and dagger?" Jordan asked.

"Funny you should say that, being we're undercover agents. I got some intel indicating the "Miles Raiders" may be involve with our sting tonight." Tyler stated.

"CPD-Gang Unit slipped me some info about the motorcycle club being protection for a drug movement. Not sure where or for whom." Carter added.

Jordan looks around for suspected counterintelligence. He then asks, "You are going tell Ford about this?"

"Not at the briefing, only our team will be purview to this," replied Tyler. The three men concluded their conversation and headed back into the building.

It's 5:30 p.m. and Happy Hour is in full swing at Kraus' Gentlemen's Club. The stage is currently occupied by a trio of dancers performing erotic events. Sasha is the main attraction of the three. Blondie and Champagne are doing their pole routines as Sasha sits in a birthing position, displaying a six-inch Cigar from her vagina. Each time she contracts her muscles, smoke emerges from her vagina and the ignited cigar lights up. The audience applauds her exotic skills of entertainment. Champagne keeps the crowd going as she slides down the pole onto a stack of quarters and consumes them inside of her. She then climbs back up the pole, spreads her legs and releases the coins from her vagina individually. The audience shouts and whistles in applauding her performance. In addition to Champagne and Sasha's performance, Blondie ends the show by balancing a twelve-ounce beer bottles on her buttocks, while clapping her butt cheeks.

Kraus sits in his office auditing his finances from the club. He could hear the patrons cheering for the dancers in a far distance. Suddenly a subtle knock came upon Kraus' side entrance door. He rose from his desk to investigate the knock and learned it was Father Terry and Jaden. Kraus opens the door, inviting his guests in. Jaden places a duffle bag of money on his dad's desk.

"Here's your laundry, pops." Jaden stated.

Kraus smiles at his son's comment as he tokes onto a cigar. He takes out a stack of one-hundred-dollar bills, places them stack by his ear and flipping each paper bill.

"Sounds like money," said Kraus.

"Clean money as always! I find it strange, you to forgetting to pick up your laundry." Terry commented.

Kraus looks over at Terry and scoffs. "You of all people, should know perception can be interpreted in many ways. I need no liabilities associated with my operation. The fact you have vagrants running around your church doesn't sit well with me. I was going to send Jaden to pick up my laundry anyway. Thanks for bringing it by, son." Kraus stated.

Jaden clears his throat and sits down before his father's desk. "Bringing your laundry is not the reason I stopped by, Pops." Jaden stated.

Jaden needed a place to store his next shipment of drugs. Kraus had a wine cellar in the basement of his club and Jaden knew it. He asked his father could he spare some space to accommodate his shipment. Kraus was hesitant to assist his son's endeavors, but agreed anyway.

"Who's attaches to this shipment?" Kraus asks.

Jaden told his father it was a business associates who would rather remain anonymous. The fact Jaden wanted to keep his business associates anonymous made Kraus even more uneasy.

"You have twenty-four hours of storage. After that, it will be the found property of CPD." Kraus stated.

Jaden nodded in agreement to his father's instructions. He then rose from his seat to exit his father's office. Father Terry stayed behind at the request of Kraus.

"What do you know about this shipment?" Kraus asks.

Father Terry chuckled and replied, "I'm just washing laundry. Dirty laundry isn't my concern." Father Terry then exits the way he and Jaden entered.

Back at the field office, ODI Agents were still in briefing. The digital clock on the wall read 6:25 p.m. Agent Ford is giving her closing remarks to the briefing.

"Listen up, we're almost done here. I need no hiccups during this op. Alpha Team will consist of Stanzell, Duncan and myself. Bravo Team will be Carter and Tyler with eyes on the UC. Jordan, we'll go off your call as the UC. Alpha Team will take command with assistance from Bravo. Charlie Company will be in charge of entry and perimeter security." Ford instructed.

Jordan looks around the duty room, examining the people he'll be putting his trust in for the undercover assignment. The feeling in his gut tells him his circle of trust is smaller than he imagines. Jordan turns his attention in preparing his gear and the ambience of the duty room return to indistinctive chatter as final preparations were made for the op.

CHAPTER TEN: TAKEN

Carter looks down at his watch and it reads 10:33 p.m. CPD and ODI personnel are staging at the Lee-Harvard Shopping Center. Agent Ford's team are finalizing preparations as Detective Carter walks up.

"You guys ready to go?" Carter asks Ford.

"My team is ready. What about your boys?" Ford replied.

"SWAT is cuing up now and patrol are establishing perimeter control before we roll out." Carter indicated.

"Good! We can do a quick brief before heading out." Ford instructed.

Ford then looks over at Jordan. He was finalizing his props for his cover as Malik St.Charles. She observed him to be deep in thought, displaying confidence for tonight's assignment. Jordan's demeanor gave Ford the assurance she needed.

"John-Sam-Nine, control." CPD Dispatch calls for Detective Carter.

"Control go ahead." Carter responded.

"One-Mary-Fourteen and assisting units are in place for execution." CPD Dispatch advised.

"Roger that!" Carter responded.

Carter informed Ford, patrol had diverted traffic and sustained an outer perimeter for execution. Jordan walks over to Carter and gives him a head gesture indicating "he's set to go". Carter nods in acknowledgement of his confidence. Agent Tyler is sitting on the front bumper of his unmarked vehicle. He watches Jordan from a short distance, observing his every move. In an agent's description of duties, life changing events can happen at any moment. Tyler didn't want to experience another brother lost in the line of duty. He gets in his vehicle and leaves the staging area. Ford began huddling up the troops for a final briefing before execution. She looks over her shoulder and observed the taillights of Agent Tyler's vehicle vanishing in the night.

Currently at Kraus' Gentlemen's Club, Jaden arrives driving a white utility van. He enters the back-parking lot of the club, which is adjacent to the door of his father's office. Jaden backs the van up to the door. Kraus was waiting to assist with unloading the product. He opens the back door of the van and observes Johnnie B possessing an AR-15 Assault Rifle.

"I see you brought help." Kraus stated.

"Pop, you of all people know you have to be ready for anything." Jaden replies.

"Let me help you with those bags ole timer." Johnnie B commented.

Kraus chuckles at Johnnie B's remark as they unload the merchandise. Kraus gave precise directions to his wine cellar. The instructions lead Johnnie B to a set of steps descending into a narrow hallway. Johnnie B noticed the door to this area was locked. Kraus whistles down at Johnnie B. He then tosses a ring with two keys attached.

"Try the one with the black casing." Kraus instructed.

Johnnie locates the key an access the door. He notices the lights to systematically illuminates as he advances the wine cellar. Johnnie B began looking around for a spot to place the product.

"Go fifteen steps, turn right and place the bags against the wall." Kraus informs Johnnie B.

Johnnie B chuckles and followed the instructions given. Kraus goes back to the van to gather more bags of the product. Upon his arrival, he'd noticed Jaden unloaded all the bags needed to be stored.

"This is it Pop! I'm taking the rest to another location. If it's anything I've learned from you, never store all your eggs in one basket." Jaden stated.

Kraus chuckles as he gathered the remaining bags and carried them to the cellar. As he walks towards the cellar, he was met by Johnnie be at the top of the stairs. Kraus paused with a stare as he looks at Johnnie B. He then scoffs and gives Johnnie the bags to take inside the cellar.

"Like I said Pops, let me get that." Johnnie stated.

"It's all yours, just be sure to store it by the wall as instructed." Kraus replies.

Johnnie B returns to the cellar, finishing the task at hand. Kraus returns to his office to claim the remaining bags. As he's about to turn the knob of his office door, Sasha enters the private hallway.

"What do you have going on tonight?" Sasha asks.

"Business!" Kraus replies.

"You should let me serve some of this cake with your business." Sasha inquires.

"That could be arrange, but for now, It's just business." Kraus implied.

Sasha scoffs at Kraus' comment and walks away in the direction of the bar area. Kraus looks around to assure no one else is in the vicinity of his office. He then enters his office with haste. Jaden is securing the back door of the van as Kraus enters his office. Kraus could hear the latching of a door after it slams shut. He then sees Jaden enter through the side entrance door of his office.

"Let's finish this shit up. I don't want anyone knowing about your product in my club." Kraus advised.

Jaden assisted his father with the remaining bags. As they exited Kraus' office, Sasha was lurking around the corner of the private hallway. She then observes Kraus and Jaden heading in the direction of the wine cellar. Sasha crept slowly at a distance as to not be detected. Her snooping lead her to the steps descending before the cellar door. Sasha could hear the voices of Kraus, Jaden and Johnnie B as she stood at the entrance of the cellar.

"Kraus, how long can we keep this product here?" Johnnie B asks.

"It appears my son didn't inform you of my instructions. Twenty-four hours of storage. After that, you will need another location to store your drugs." Kraus advised.

"Drugs, What the fuck?" Sasha whispers to herself. She then runs up the flight of stairs and heads to the female dressing room. Within a minute, she enters the dressing room and began twisting the combination to her locker. Seconds later, she opens the compartment and retrieves her cellphone. Sasha clicks the keypad icon and dials a number unassisted to her contacts. After three long rings, a male's voice answers the open line.

"Who tis'" The Male answers.

"This Sasha. The drugs are here"

"Bitch you better be right!" The Male replies in an authoritative voice.

The line disconnects and Sasha places her phone back into the locker. She closes her eyes and takes in a deep breath, slowly exhaling to calm her nerves. "What the fuck I've gotten myself into?" She slams her fist into the locker with a downward strike. "Fuck, fuck, fuck!" She utters, while striking the locker again.

Meanwhile, Jaden and Johnnie B are standing in the back-parking lot adjacent to Kraus' office. Johnnie B enters the van, while Jaden is saying goodbye to Kraus.

"Pop don't worry, I'll get this off your hands by morning." Jaden promised.

Kraus nodded and walked back into his office, closing the door behind him. He then sits at his desk as he hears the van driving off.

Back at the staging site of Lee-Harvard shopping Center, Agent Ford prepares her team for departure onto the Juva De. Jordan walks over and saddles upon a "1953 Indian Road-master". The all black motorcycle was decked out with leather seats and roaring silver pipes.

The bike roared as Jordan started her up and purred as her engine idled.

"Where did you find this beauty?" Carter asks.

"Got her through an auction in Akron, two years ago." Jordan replied.

"To be honest, I never knew you could play the part. Carter stated.

Jordan chuckles and replies, "it's a lot of shit you don't know about me."

The Road-master roars again as Jordan rides off, leaving Carter standing in awe. Stanzell walks up and slaps Carter on his back shoulder.

"Let's go, time to roll!" Stanzell stated.

Meanwhile, Pam was at home grading class work from her students. She removes her wire frame glasses to rub her eyes and places them back upon her face. A sudden burst of wind rattles the windows, startling Pam and breaking her focus. She takes a deep breath and reaches for her glass of Merlot. Drinking half of its contents, Pam places the glass back on the night stand and returns to grading papers. A few minutes goes by, allowing Pam to be fully engulfed into her work. Only to be startled again, this time from the loud buzzing of her cellphone. She picks up the device and sees Miles' number.

"What do you want at this hour?" Pam answered jokingly.

"My Mom's and I were thinking about stopping by." Miles replied.

"Debra in town? When did she get in?" Pam asks excitingly.

"This morning, I would have called you earlier, but I became so busy with work." Miles stated.

"Ok, come on by. I need a break from grading these papers anyway." Pam exclaims.

"Cool, we'll see you in twenty." Miles said.

"Okay, see you then!" Pam replies.

Pam ended her call with Miles. She then walks into her bedroom closet to find some presentable clothing to wear.

Currently at the Juva De, Jordan is arriving in front of the premises. He parks his bike on the main drag of Harvard Avenue. "Black Beauty" roars once more before he shuts her off. As he dismounts his bike, Jordan acknowledges the compliments about "Black Beauty" from onlookers. He secures his helmet to the bike and enters the club.

Jordan asks the outside security guard to keep an eye on his bike as he slides him a "Benjamin" for his efforts. The bouncer gives Jordan a head nod as he allows him entry into the establishment. The club's atmosphere presented a Gangster-Hip Hop vibe on this night, totally different from Jordan's initial visit. He approaches the bar and claims a vacant seat in front of a barmaid. The barmaid is wiping down the counter as Jordan encounters her personal space.

"Anyone sitting here?" Jordan asks.

"You!" The barmaid stated.

"Cool!" Jordan replied.

"What are you drinking?" The Barmaid asks.

"Double shot of Vodka on the rocks. Wait, make that a Double of Jaimie. I want to feel myself tonight." Jordan stated.

The barmaid chuckled as she began preparing Jordan's drink. He looks over his shoulder and sees Agent Duncan walking in with Stanzell. The two glanced at Jordan and headed for a nearby table. They selected a one with unobstructed viewpoints to exits and entrances of the club. Jordan's turns back around as the barmaid is placing his drink before him. He takes a sip of his drink, swirling its contents around in his mouth and then swallows it.

"Not bad, not bad at all." Jordan stated.

"It's unusual to see a black man sipping Jameson. You Black-Irish or something?" The Barmaid asks jokingly.

"Oh, I'm something. I can be many things should you be willing to find out." Jordan stated.

"We'll see!" Chuckles the Barmaid. She then walks off to service other customers at the bar.

Jordan smiles at the barmaid's comment. He watches her rounds ass sways from side to side in slow-motion affect. Suddenly, the vibration from his cellphone breaks his concentration. Jordan retrieves it from the bar and reads a text from Ford.

"How we looking inside?" Ford text.

"We good. My back up is here!" Jordan text back.

Outside of the Juva De, Tyler sat alone in his unmark, monitoring radio traffic of the op. He puffs on a cigar and scans the area for counterintelligence. Tyler looks onto the dashboard and sees his cellphone vibrating from a text.

"Bro, stay frosty. I need your support on this one." Jordan text.

"No worries, I got you Lil' bro." Tyler text back.

Jordan was reading Tyler's text as the barmaid return to check on him. She raised the bottle of Jameson, indicating a refill of his drink. Jordan nods, as affirmation to refill his glass. The barmaid pours slow, this time doubling his original double. She then places a second glass next to his and pours a double for herself. The two toast glasses as the barmaid downs her drink in one setting, leaving Jordan sipping on his.

"Scary!" Jordan stated.

"Yeah, how so?" Barmaid asks.

"Last time I witnessed a woman do that, I had to put in extra work." Jordan said.

"Well, I hope your back is ready." Replies the Barmaid. She smiles and then walks away again to assist other customers. This time she looks back over her shoulder and winks at Jordan.

Back at the Jordan's home, Pam here's the doorbell ring. "Shit, they got here quick. Miles said fifteen minutes." Pam utters. She rushes downstairs which lead to the front door. Pam was still shaken from what happened a few days ago, so she didn't turn on additional lights to give away her location in the house. As Pam peeps through her curtains adjacent to the front door, she's able to see it Miles and Debra.

"Girl, open the door. It's your aunt Debra!"

"And Miles!"

Pam chuckled as she unlocked her door and invited them in. She then peers out of the front door after Miles and Debra entered, assuring no one was watching her house. Upon seeing nothing, Pam closes the door and walks her family into the den area.

"Look at you, thin shaping and shit. You need some meat on those bones." Debra said.

"Momma, all black women don't have to be round. My cousin looks good!" Miles commented.

"You calling your Momma fat? Don't have me slap the shit out of you. With your metro-dressing ass." Debra replies.

Pam stands across from Miles with her mouth open and smiling at her aunt's comment. The days of when she talks mess to them as kids are coming back as memories. Pam invites her family to make themselves comfortable.

"Auntie, what would you like to drink?" Pam asks.

"Some Hen-Hen if you have it." Replied Debra.

"I don't have any Hennessy, but James have Jameson in the covered." Pam stated.

"Jameson, isn't that a white man's whiskey." Debra asks.

"Auntie, I don't know. I just know it's something he likes drinking." Pam says with a chuckle.

"Oh well, pour me a shot or two. Beggars can't be choosers." Debra replies.

"Cousin, let me get one too?" Miles requested.

Pam rises from her lazy-boy recliner and walks into the kitchen to make drinks for her guests. Aunt Debra and Cousin Miles began chattering amongst themselves in the absence of Pam.

11:30 p.m., operation "Juva De" is in full swing. Agent Ford and Detective Carter are managing the operations from a blacked-out utility van. Agent Tyler remains alone in his unmark vehicle, while SWAT is at their secondary staging location, the parking lot of JFK High School.

Ford transmit across her radio requesting a comms-check, "All units, this is Agent Ford, report status checks."

"Duncan and Stanzell, code four."

"Jordan code four, nothing to report."

"Charlie Company, code four, perimeter secure."

"SWAT Command, code four, units standing by for instructions."

"Roger that!" Agent Ford responded.

While inside the Juva De, Jordan pans the club for the Presence of Johnnie B and Jaden. He finds them to be nowhere in sight. The genre of clientele fits the music being played as more and more people enters the club.

"Yo Jay, any signs of your boy?" Duncan asks by way of earwigs.

"Negative. I'm wondering if he's going to show!" Jordan responded.

"No worries, he and Jaden will show." Tyler commented by earwig.

Unbeknownst to the team, Jaden and Johnnie B are less than twenty minutes away. Johnnie B texts his security staff to assure everything is good for their arrival. The bouncer, manning the front entrance of the club receives Johnnie B's text.

"We're about fifteen minutes out." Johnnie B's text.

"All good to arrive." The bouncer text back.

Back at the Jordan's home, Pam returns from the kitchen with drinks for Miles and Debra.

"I hope yawl like my libations?" Pam stated.

"Girl, stop being bougie and come toast a drink with your Auntie."

Pam handed Debra and Miles their drinks, toasting to a small reunion as they conversed about old times. Miles couldn't stop laughing upon the mentioning of their memories. Pam picks up a pillow and throws it at him as they bonded, while Aunt Debra facilitated their stories.

Currently on scene, a CPD unit advises a white utility van headed towards the Juva De. Patrol, suspects it may be Johnnie B and Jaden. As the van approaches the alleyway adjacent to the club, Tyler is able to identify its passenger.

"Lincoln 257 to mobile command, the passenger of said vehicle is identified as Johnnie B. I say again, I have a positive on the passenger as Johnnie B." Tyler reported.

"All units be ready to move upon Agent Jordan's call." Ford instructed.

Jaden turns into an alley adjoining the Juva De and parks next to the club's emergency door. Agent Ford advises her Video Tech to zoom in on the van.

"Team be advised, we have video confirmation of Johnnie B exiting the van." Ford reported.

Johnnie B unlocks the emergency door and enters the club. Jaden, whose identity hasn't been confirmed, remains in the van.

"Do we have confirmation on the driver?" SWAT Commander asks.

"Negative, driver has not been identified." Ford responded.

Johnnie B meets his security personnel in the east stairwell of the club. They return back to the van and retrieve three of the remaining six bags of drugs. Jaden still remains in the van as Johnnie B and his men reenters the club. They take the stairwell leading to the back door of the club's kitchen. Johnnie B instructs his men to place the bags upon the metal counter.

"Wait here, I'll be right back." Johnnie instructed.

Johnnie B exits the kitchen leading into the bar and dance area. Jordan is sitting at the bar as he makes his entrance. For the moment, Johnnie B doesn't notice Jordan sitting at the bar. He's enticed by the club vibe and the patrons having fun.

Jordan notices Johnnie B at the end of the bar and shortly thereafter, Johnnie B notices Jordan. Surprised of Jordan's presence, Johnnie B turns and reenters the kitchen. Jordan noticed Johnnie B's immediate departure and quickly follows after him. Agents Duncan and Stanzell observes Jordan's abrupt movement and trails his steps.

"Heads up, we have movement. Jordan is following someone into the kitchen." Duncan radioed.

Suddenly, sounds of gun shots came from the kitchen area. Patrons began to scatter as Duncan and Stanzell approached with their guns drawn.

"Shots fired; shots fired. Roll SWAT, now!" Stanzell instructed.

As Stanzell and Duncan enters the kitchen, they observe Jordan shooting from behind a metal door at two assailants. Duncan and Stanzell trained their weapons onto the assailants as they saw their colleague in eminent distress. Seconds later, the assailants were neutralized.

Ford, accompanied by Carter and Tyler enters the kitchen from the club area. They find Jordan, Duncan and Stanzell standing over the bodies of two dead assailants.

"What happened here?" Ford questioned.

"I followed Johnnie B into the kitchen and was ambushed with gunfire by these two. Jordan explains as he pointed at the dead assailants.

"We came in after hearing gunshots and found the assailants shooting at Jordan." Duncan advised.

"Where the fuck is Johnnie B?" Carter interrupts.

"He went out the emergency exit." Jordan replies.

Before Carter could radio assisting units, a series of gunshot ranged out from the adjacent alley. It was the mixture of semi and automatic weapons sounding off continuously.

"CPD SWAT, what's your status?" Carter requested.

"We're taking heavy fire. I repeat, heavy fire!"

Onlookers from outside of the club, watched muzzle flashes and rapid sounds of gunfire from the alley adjoining Juva De. The event went on for minutes until Ford radioed for seize fire. Ford's team exited from the emergency entrance, establishing a secured perimeter of the van. CPD SWAT intersects Ford's perimeter to access the van. SWAT cleared the van and observed no suspects inside. Johnnie B and Jaden had escaped, leaving the remaining bags of drugs inside the van.

"Control, John-Sam-Nine." Carter calls out.

"John-Sam-Nine." Control responded.

"I need a code red. I say again, a code red for two armed suspects. Give me a two-mile radius of the Juva De." Carter instructed.

"Copy, John-Sam-Nine." Control responded.

At this time, Jaden and Johnnie B are cutting through residential backyards to find an escape route. They come across a Datsun 310 on a residential street. Johnnie B punched the driver side lock to gain access. Once inside, he unlocks the passenger door for Jaden. Seconds later, the vehicle is hot wired and the two suspects are in the wind. Jaden then takes out his cell to call Kraus, but his phone rings to voicemail on several attempts. He leaves Kraus a text to contact him.

"Pops, call me back. CPD ambushed us at the club. Keep the remaining product at your spot until I can retrieve it later."

During The time of Jaden's distress, Kraus was sexing Sasha in his office. She was moaning intensely as he had her bent over on his desk.

"Pound that kitty, daddy. Make her meow for you!" Sasha moaned.

The impact from Kraus' thrust, made Sasha's D-cups knock his phone off the stand. The digital screen of the phone became visible to Sasha as she continued to moan. Her loud cries distracted Kraus, allowing her to read his text message from Jaden. Kraus pulls himself out of Sasha and skeets upon her back.

"I liked your expression upon my back. It was nice and warm!" Sasha stated as she turns around.

"Yeah, the kitty cat wasn't bad either." Kraus responded. The lit screen from Kraus' cellphone catches his attention. "What the fuck did you do to my desk?" He asked.

"That cock of yours, caused these tits to knock things over." Sasha replies while grabbing her breasts.

Kraus scoffs at Sasha's comment. He then tells her to get dress and leave his office. Sasha smirks a grin and walks out naked. Kraus stares at her ass, watching it sway from side to side. He then closes the door and calls his son to find out what he wanted.

"What's up Pops." Jaden answers.

"You tell me! Where are you?" Kraus asks.

"Headed to you." Jaden stated.

"Negative, go to St. Terry's. I'll contact you later." Kraus instructed.

Jaden instructed Johnnie B to make their route onto the highway. He gave directions to Saint Terry's Catholic Church.

"Take the Broadway exit and we'll come through the back way of East 131 Street." Jaden stated.

Johnnie nodded, indicating he understood the directions. As he continued driving, Jaden began pondering what went wrong. To Jaden, Saint Terry's Catholic Church was a spot he could drop a lid on his problems and process the outcome. Jaden opened his contacts to Father Terry's number. He then sends him a text message about his arrival.

"I'm on my way to the church. Me and a friend need a safe heaven. Hit me back!" Jaden text.

Johnnie B looked over at Jaden, wanting to tell him about Jordan and how he may be related to the shooting. He felt responsible on how things went down. Jaden was lost in thought, concerned about the abandoned shipment of drugs.

Back at the Gentlemen's Club, Kraus is on the phone with Father Terry. He informs him of Jaden's situation and asks for safe refuge for his son.

"Look Terry, I know we're not the best of friends and poor at being business partners. I'm asking this favor for my son." Kraus exclaims.

"I'll look out for your son, but what about this friend he's bringing. I received a text from him stating he's on his way with someone." Terry stated.

"He's some Haitian fuck, I can care less for. You do what you can for my son, are we clear!" Kraus advised.

"Consider it handled." Terry replies.

He then prepares for the arrival of Jaden and Johnnie B. Worried he may be raided by law enforcement, Kraus rushes to his wine cellar to relocate Jaden's drugs. As he quickly entered the cellar, Kraus began transferring the drugs into a secret room where he hid stacks of money and gambling equipment. After multiple trips from moving the drugs, Kraus looks down at his watch and it reads 12:15 am. He began to secure his hidden storage, but is interrupted by Caribbean Jay.

"You can leave the door open." Jay stated.

"You have no idea, who you're fucking with." Kraus stated as he turns around slowly with his hands raised.

"See, that's where you're wrong. I do know you and your bitch-ass son." Jay responded.

"Should have known I can't trust a bitch! What's up Sasha, dick wasn't good enough? You had to bring someone to rob me?" Kraus stated.

Sasha begins to shout insults at Kraus, but Jay yields her message. He then requested Kraus' keys to his Mercedes. Kraus tosses them onto the floor.

"Bitch, get the keys." Jay demanded Sasha.

"Where did you and I meet, for you to know me?" Kraus asks.

"We didn't, but you knew my family and you killed my cousin." Caribbean Jay stated.

Jay pulls the trigger of his Desert eagle and watched its bullets pierced the body of Kraus. Jay walks over to Kraus' body and extends another bullet into his head. Kraus laid lifeless as Jay and Sasha emptied his hidden storage. Jay even took Kraus' illegal gambling money, loading everything into his black Tahoe. He gave Sasha a hundred grand of Kraus' money and told her to take the Mercedes as a gift. Jay then leaves Kraus' body to be found as an indication of a robbery. Sasha stays behind to gather all her belongings as she had no intentions of coming back.

"Thanks for your help, I'll catch you around." Jay stated as he said his goodbyes.

Currently at the Juva De, the Coroner is wrapping up his investigation, while CPD Crime Techs are still categorizing evidence. Ensue of their duties, a technician uncovers the escape route of Johnnie B and Jaden. It led him to a residential street where the Datsun-310 was stolen. The Crime Tech further identifies a key housing from a car door. He expects it been dislodged during an attempt to steal a vehicle.

"Charlie-Tom-15 to John-Sam-Nine." The technician calls out.

"Go for John-Sam-Nine." Carter responded.

"I've located a lock casing on the street. It appears to have been punched from something. I'm guessing a vehicle." The technician stated.

Carter instructed a few uniformed officers to canvas the area where the technician found the lock casing. He'd hope someone could have seen their suspects and maybe identify their direction of travel. At this point, Carter needed something to break in this case. The officer's assisting in canvassing had little experience with interviewing witness'. Agent Ford needed real-time evidence fast, so she called in a favor from a close contact of the "Joint Terrorism Task Force". She used her satellite phone, given to her for eminent situations.

"Tango-Foxtrot-269, this is Charlie-1-5-6." Ford stated.

"Charlie-1-5-6, go." Unknown voice advised.

"I need to locate a vehicle leaving a specific area within the last hour." Ford requested.

"Location you're requesting from?" Unknown voice asks.

"State-Log: 179.388 / Latitude: 41.368589 / Longitude: 81.96595." Ford advised.

"Roger that, standby." Unknown voice replies.

The unknown voice returns information to Ford, advising the vehicle had left the request area thirty minutes ago and is currently at the location of Saint Terry's Catholic Church. Ford informs her team of the suspects location. She and accompanied officers head to the church of Father Terry's, hoping to find their suspects.

Currently at Saint Terry's Catholic Church, Jaden tells Father Terry what happened at the club. Johnnie's conscious begins to get the best of him, forcing a confession as to why things went south.

"Jaden, I didn't say this before due to our situation. When I took the drugs inside the club, I saw a familiar face." Johnnie B explains.

"Who?" Jaden asked.

"Malik St. Charles!" Johnnie B replied.

"That Trini-bastard?" Jaden asked angrily.

"I went back into the kitchen and down the east stairwell into ally. When I reach the van and saw SWAT, I panicked and started shooting. Johnnie exclaims.

"You think he's 5-0?" Jaden asks.

"Not sure, but I do know he and Caribbean Jay are partners." Johnnie B stated.

Jaden began pondering the pieces of this unraveling puzzle. He knew Caribbean Jay was "Zoe-Pound", but wasn't sure how Malik St. Charles and Caribbean Jay was related. Just then a shadow figure appeared at the entrance of the sanctuary. Jaden and Johnnie B didn't notice him because he stood at their backs.

"Excuse me gentlemen, I have a guest to attend. Wait here!" Father Terry advised.

Terry met with his guests, while Jaden and Johnnie B continued talking amongst themselves. After about five minutes, Father Terry returned.

"Gentlemen, I have some new and pertinent information for you both. Let's go to my office." Father Terry advises.

Jaden and Johnnie B followed Terry to his office as requested. Upon entering, Jaden noticed Sasha bonded to a chair and gagged. Sasha failed to leave the club before the arrival of Father Terry's goons. Terry sent them to retrieve Kraus, but they were too late. The goons found Kraus dead, along with the money and dope missing. They grabbed Sasha instead and brought her to Father Terry for questioning. The goons began working Sasha over and over until she was bloody. After 15 minutes of torture, Father Terry told his men to stop. Sasha's face was pummeled with her right eye closed shut and blood dripping from her mouth.

"My child, I'm sure by now, this person can't be that much of importance to you." Father Terry advises.

Sasha began to utter words of confession to Father Terry. "It was Caribbean Jay. He killed Kraus, because Kraus killed his cousin." Sasha continued her confession in a weak and trembling voice. "The girl in the news, three or four years ago. She was the daughter of a cop. Caribbean Jay said Kraus had her killed. That's why he killed him." Sasha exclaims before passing out.

"Wake that bitch up, she knows more than that!" Jaden shouted.

"Quiet down!" Father Terry commanded.

Father Terry remembers the story Sasha referenced. He further remembered Kraus ordering a hit on Sergeant Jordan and his family. He retrieved an old news article from his desk drawer with the picture of Jordan. Father Terry shows the clipping to Jaden and Johnnie B. Jaden didn't recognize him, but Johnnie B did. Johnnie eyes widen when seeing the photo.

"That's, that's Malik St. Charles. He and Caribbean Jay are boys." Johnnie B exclaims.

Father Terry removes a .38 caliber revolver from his cloth and shoots Johnnie B in the head. Jaden gasp and yells at Father Terry.

"Why the fuck you did that?" Jaden asks in distress.

"Because he's a snitch. How you think CPD got on to you? Thanks to Narcotics-Detective Smith, I solve your snitch problem. Detective, get over to the Jordan's house, I'm going to needs some leverage to create some distance."

Just as law enforcement personnel were breaching the church entrances; Father Terry, Jaden and Detective Smith were making their escape by way of an underground tunnel. The route took them outside of police perimeters and to a pair of vehicles available for their escape. Father Terry and Jaden entered one vehicle, while Detective Smith drove off in another. Smith set his route in accordance to the Jordan's residence.

Upon entry of St. Terry's church, Ford and the other law enforcement personnel found the body of Johnnie B. Sasha was barely alive from her beating. Agent Duncan was tapping her on the cheek for a response.

Ma'am, are you ok? Can you hear me, ma'am? Duncan asks.

Sasha looks around the room and smiles, because she's still alive. She sees Johnnie B's body adjacent from her location and began to whimper, followed by short intervals of cries.

"Ma'am, ma'am! What's wrong? How can I help?" Duncan asks.

"Let me talk to her." Jordan requested.

Duncan steps back and allows Jordan to do his thing. He brings Sasha a cup of water to sip on. Coaching her to take small sips and relax before speaking. He then takes a knee before her, allowing Sasha to look at him as she began to speak. Jordan observed her body to involuntary shake and her voice to tremble while composing each word.

"He-beat-me, but I told him nothing." Sasha said in her final gasping voice.

Jordan watches Sasha die before he could extract any information. He checked her carotid artery for a pulse and felt nothing. Duncan radioed for a Coroner to their location. She requested a uniform officer to tape off the area of Johnnie B and Sasha as the primary crime scene. Jordan retrieve his phone to text Caribbean Jay.

"Nephew, I found Johnnie B dead at the church. Hit me back! Jordan text.

Caribbean Jay was currently crossing into the State of Kentucky from Ohio, when he received Jordan's text. Conscious of being tracked, Jay turned his cellphone off.

For minutes, Jordan stares at his phone waiting for a text, but no text appeared from Jay. Finally, he places his phone away and assist the agents in searching for evidence.

Meanwhile at the Jordan's home, Pam is still entertaining her aunt and cousin. She notices the lights to flicker in short intervals. Pam looks over at Miles with a curious look upon her face. Aunt Debra begins to joke about the situation.

"Girl, don't tell me you didn't pay the light bill." Debra stated jokingly.

Pam chuckled in discomfort, for she knew her bills weren't the issue. She began to have thoughts about the mysterious vehicle a few days ago. Pam then looks at Miles with concern. Before Miles could respond to Pam's reaction, the lights went out.

"I hope you have an extra fuse." Debra says jokingly, again.

Pam leaves Miles and Debra in the den as she felt her way to the kitchen. She searched through the kitchen drawers to locate a flashlight and the fuse. "Come on. It has to be here somewhere," she said out loud.

Pam becomes startled as a hand is placed across her mouth. It was Miles with Debra standing behind him. He places his right index finger to his lips, indicating to be quiet as he slowly removes his left hand from Pam's mouth.

"I don't think it's a fuse. I heard something outside and wanted to make sure you were ok." Miles whispered.

"I'm fine," Pam whispers back.

Suddenly, a faint sound of glass breaking came from the den area. Miles went for his weapon but was struck by a bullet in his shoulder. He falls back against the kitchen wall and slides down to the floor. Miles looks over and finds his mother laying adjacent to him, dead. The bullet which struck Miles, passed through his mother's body after killing her. A shadow figure inters the kitchen and finishes his assault onto Miles, shooting him in the head. Pam takes off running through the house to escape her attacker, but runs into another assailant who renders her unconscious.

Detective Carter receives a phone call from dispatch informing the murder of Kraus at his Club. He informs Agent Ford he needed to assist homicide with another investigation. Ford acknowledges his departure and advises she would take over the scene.

"What do you think?" Ford asks Jordan.

"I think we're fuck. Father Terry is in the wind and We have two dead bodies to follow up on." Jordan said.

Ford wasn't happy with the results, but Jordan was right. All they had was some dope and no one to connect it to. Johnnie B, Sasha and now Kraus was listed as dead. If the team wanted to learn more of what happened tonight, they would need to find Father Terry. As protocol, Agent Ford turn the scene over to the County Coroner.
Death-Investigator Korda, arrives on scene to declare the official time of death.

"Hey Korda, sorry to have pulled you out of bed." Jordan apologizes.

"No worries, I was at the office when this call came out. Well, this is a simple case of murder and the cause of death seems obvious." Korda stated.

"How can you tell? They both weren't killed the same." Jordan indicates.

"Easily, blunt force trauma and gunshot wound. Contusion upon the female victim's face are from severe blows, which indicates brain hemorrhaging. Our male victim appears to have a bullet to the forehead, which indicates the obvious. I'll know more after autopsy." Korda explains.

Jordan nods and then informs Ford of the preliminary findings, stating the coroner will have conclusive results after the autopsy. Ford acknowledges his debrief and advises him to go home. Jordan leaves the scene but has no intentions of going home right away.

"Nephew, its important. Hit me back, we need to talk!" Jordan shoots Jay another text before leaving the crime scene.

Three hours later, Jordan arrives at home. He notices the front door ajar with no working lights. Jordan takes out his weapon and pocket flashlights upon entering his home. Examining his surroundings before advancing, Jordan slowly walks into the den area and locates the fuse box. He then flicks a switch to illuminates the house. At his surprise, Jordan observes the lifeless body of Pam's aunt. He further walks into the kitchen and finds the body of Miles. Fearing for Pam's safety, Jordan began clearing the house in search of her. As several minutes elapsed, Jordan found no signs of Pam. He then called the only person he could trust.

Agent Tyler is currently at home cooking a midnight dinner for his girlfriend. He checks on the perfection of his signature stir-fried rice and steak. "It's almost ready." Tyler chuckles as he speaks out loud. He then turns the flame down to a simmer, allowing the ingredients to marinate. Suddenly, Tyler hears the sounds of his cellphone buzzing from the kitchen counter. Curious of the call, he walks over to the counter and learn it's Jordan buzzing his phone. Tyler answers-

"Bro, they took her. They took Pam. THEY TOOK MY WIFE!" Jordan shouts through the phone.

Jordan begins crying as he collapses to his knees. Tyler holds the phone in silence, feeling defenseless in aiding his partner as he listens on the other end. Now that their first mission as a team is complete; ODI agents Tyler, Ford, Duncan and Stanzell will have to come together and help Jordan. The disappearance of Pam is a mystery to them all, and Its going to take everyone in this quest to find her.